W9-AXR-324

Stumptown Kid

Stumptown Kid

Property of
Resurrection Lutheran Academy

written by Carol Gorman
and Ron J. Findley

PEACHTREE
ATLANTA

Published by
PEACHTREE PUBLISHERS
1700 Chattahoochee Avenue
Atlanta, Georgia 30318-2112

www.peachtree-online.com

Text © 2005 by Carol Gorman and Ron J. Findley

First trade paperback edition published April 2007

All rights reserved. No part of this publication may be reproduced, stored in a
retrieval system, or transmitted in any form or by any means—electronic,
mechanical, photocopy, recording, or any other—except for brief quotations in
printed reviews, without the prior permission of the publisher.

Cover design by Loraine M. Joyner
Book design by Melanie McMahon Ives

Manufactured in United States of America

10 9 8 7 6 5 4 3 (hardcover)
10 9 8 7 6 5 4 3 2 (trade paperback)

Background baseball player photo courtesy of the Library of Congress, Prints and
Photographs Division, George Grantham Bain Collection.

Library of Congress Cataloging-in-Publication Data

Gorman, Carol.
 Stumptown kid / written by Carol Gorman and Ron J. Findley.-- 1st ed.
  p. cm.
 Summary: In a small Iowa town in 1952, eleven-year-old Charlie Nebraska, whose
father died in the Korean War, learns the meanings of both racism and heroism
when he befriends a black man who had played baseball in the Negro Leagues.
 ISBN 13: 978-1-56145-337-5 / ISBN 10: 1-56145-337-4 (hardcover)
 ISBN 13: 978-1-56145-412-9 / ISBN 10: 1-56145-412-5 (paperback)
 [1. Baseball--Fiction. 2. Coaching (Athletics)--Fiction. 3. Prejudices--Fiction. 4.
African Americans--Fiction. 5. Single-parent families--Fiction. 6. Iowa--History--20th
century--Fiction.] I. Findley, Ron J. II. Title.

 PZ7.G6693St 2005
 [Fic]--dc22

                          2004019835

*With love to my first writing teacher,
my best friend, and husband,
Ed Gorman*

—C. G.

*To my children, Jeff and Kris,
and to my grandchildren—
Ashley, Haley, Adam, Aubrey, and Hannah*

—R. J. F.

Acknowledgments

We wish to thank Art Pennington, former Negro
League star, for allowing us to interview him about
his experiences.

Thanks also to Nova Dannels at the Cedar Rapids
History Center for sharing her knowledge of Stump Town,
the egg-buying station, and other points of interest in the
Cedar Rapids area in the early 1950s.

And finally, thanks to our editor, Lisa Banim,
for believing in our story.

Chapter One

Holden, Iowa, 1952

First time I laid eyes on Luther Peale, I hardly
noticed him. That was surprising right there,
because there weren't any colored folks living in
Holden, Iowa. Fact is, I could probably have counted
on two hands the number of colored people I'd seen in
my whole life.

He came walking into the park at the beginning of
Wildcat tryouts. He looked about as old as my friend
Will's brother, who's twenty-three, and he had on a
baseball cap and clothes that seemed pretty wore out.
He set a big sack down on the bleacher, leaned against
the backstop, and watched.

His dark skin and his old gray clothes stood out
against the bright green grass all around him. A lot of
the guys looked over, curious about him being colored
and all. But no one said nothing.

I didn't think much about him at the time. My mind was fixed on doing as good as I could so Coach Hennessey would pick me for the team.

The Wildcats are a baseball team for eleven and twelve year olds, sponsored by Gamble's Shoe Store. Every guy I know wants to play with them. They don't always win, but more often than not, they do.

The tall man holding a clipboard yelled at us guys to come over. "I'm Coach Hennessey," he said, like that was necessary. "This is my assistant coach, Harv Small. I take it all you boys put your name on the sign-up sheet, right?" Nobody said different, so he went on. "First thing we do is see how you run."

He stopped and looked us over, maybe twenty-five guys, like we were a bunch of horses he might buy. "Come on," he said finally.

My friend, Will Draft, was trying out, too. He slapped me on the back. "Good luck, Charlie," he said, squinting in the bright sunshine.

"Thanks," I said. "Same to you."

"Well, well, look who's here," a voice called out behind me. "The girls from Stumptown."

I didn't have to turn around to know who was talking. Brad Lobo's always nasty, especially to the guys from Stumptown. He's twelve but as big as most fourteen year olds. He always wears shirts kind of tight, and he's got some muscles in his arms that he seems real proud of. He's a year ahead of me in school and played for the Wildcats last year. He was already on the team, but he probably figured he'd strut around at tryouts, showing off those muscles, trying to make us more nervous than we already were.

Well, I'll tell you the truth, he was doing a good job.

Lobo thinks he's a hotshot, but I have to admit he's a good ball player—third baseman, usually—one of the best the Wildcats got. His mouth is even bigger than his talent, though, let's put it that way. And he has a mean streak as wide as a country road. You can almost see the nastiness boil up inside of him and shoot out of those shiny little eyes.

I might've had a few choice words for him right then, but I really wanted to get on the team. And besides, I wasn't partial to getting killed. So I kept my mouth shut and Will did, too.

I bet all of the guys' hearts were clomping hard like mine. Playing for the Wildcats had been in my head for two years. We went to every game, me, Will, and sometimes Eileen McNally. Last year I'd started dreaming about playing for them. I'd wake up in a sweat, real excited, and it would take me a long time to get back to sleep.

We followed Coach Hennessey to the outfield. Somebody had mowed the grass in the park, and it smelled sweet and summery. Coach plodded along ahead of us, and I watched him. He's a famous guy around here. He played ball at Holden High a while back and everybody still talks about his games. He was that good. He got a baseball scholarship to the state university but hurt his leg and had to drop out. He still looks real strong, though. I heard he lifts weights a lot. He has a job at the meatpacking plant over at Cedar Rapids and got married to the mayor's daughter. Like I said, he's a winning coach, so he gets respect. He's treated almost like a movie star around Holden.

Coach Hennessey stopped in the outfield. "You guys'll start on the chalk line here," he told us. He kicked his foot at the white mark in the grass. "Harv and I are gonna stand a hundred and twenty foot away at another chalk line. I'll raise my arm. When I lower it, two of you'll start running. We'll give you your times and get your names down there. Got it?"

"If they didn't, they're too feeble-minded for the team, Coach," Lobo called out.

"You tell 'em, Lobo," Hennessey said. He and Lobo grinned at each other like they were buddies. Then Hennessey and Coach Small walked a ways out to the mark. Lobo strutted after them like a turkey who'd made it to the day after Thanksgiving. About halfway, he turned back to smirk at us.

We were going to have to run right past him. I took a big breath, wishing the butterflies in my stomach would settle down. Why did Lobo have to show up? I tried to take some breaths, deep and slow, to calm myself. But it didn't work. I was starting to sweat, and it wasn't just because it was a hot day. My armpits were damp, and my shirt grabbed on to my skin.

I wanted to get the running part over with. Maybe it would help my nerves. So I stepped up to the chalk line first. Will came up, too.

I'd brought my dad's old glove with me. I wore it at my waist like the other guys, my belt looped through it. I slid the glove around to the back so it wouldn't get in the way of my arms when I ran.

My dad was a real good runner in high school, Mom says. Grandma Nebraska has some pictures of him from when he was sixteen. In one of them he's standing on the pitcher's mound. He's thin and has brown hair like mine, and he's looking real intense, winding up for the pitch. Mom says I look more like him every day.

Dad was a hero in Korea. The Army says he died there almost two years ago. Mom didn't open the casket that was sent from Korea, so I wasn't so sure he was really dead. But I'd changed my mind about that a hundred times.

Today I didn't have an opinion. If Dad *was* dead, maybe he was watching me, seeing how I looked like him. Maybe he'd help me do good at the tryouts.

Help me run fast, Dad, I told him in my head. *If you're dead, I hope you're allowed to do things like that.*

Me and Will looked at each other and nodded. Will isn't a big talker, but his eyes are the blue of a shallow pool, and you can see everything that's going on inside him. Right now he was feeling nervous. Will's usually real steady, though, so he was in control.

"Try hard not to trip!" Lobo yelled at us. He wore a big sneer on his face.

Coach Hennessey put his arm up and sliced it down through the air. We took off.

Lobo hooted. "Look at 'em! They run like a couple o' sissies!" he hollered as we passed him. I tried to block out his words.

Will's a fast runner, and I'm not bad. He crossed the line just ahead of me. We gave the coaches our names and they wrote down our times.

I didn't feel like walking back past Lobo. I jerked my head sideways, signaling Will to move off a ways with me.

We watched the rest of the runners. Lobo shouted more mean stuff to some of the slower guys.

"I really wish Lobo hadn't shown up," I said to Will.

"Block him out of your mind," Will said. "Put up a wall between you and him."

Like I said, Will's real steady.

Me and Will's times were about average with the others.

Next Coach Hennessey divided us into two groups. "Boys on the right go with Coach Small. Rest come with me."

Will was in the other group. He held up an index finger in a little wave and moved off with Coach Small and about a dozen of the guys.

Of course Lobo hung back with his pal, Coach Hennessey. Coach said he was going to test our catching and throwing. I took my glove off my belt so I'd be ready. He had gloves for the guys who hadn't brought their own.

"We'll see how you do with fly balls," Coach said. "I'll go back to home plate and hit you some fungoes. You," he said, pointing at me, "take left field." He pointed at two other boys. "You guys, center and right."

Coach Hennessey strode back to home. That's when I noticed the colored man again. He was sitting in the bleachers behind the backstop now, his elbows resting on his knees, watching us. The big sack lay on the seat next to him.

Coach took a long, slender bat and threw the ball in the air. The first hit was to me. I saw the ball arc into the sky and fly right for me.

"Here it comes, Stumptown!" Lobo hollered from behind the guy at center field. "Don't blow it!"

I took a few steps forward and reached up to pluck it out of the air. The ball landed right behind me.

Lobo roared. "Good one, Stumptown! Your mother would be proud."

My face went hot. I was so mad at Lobo. But I was even madder at myself. How could I let him get to me like that? I usually do okay at fielding fly balls.

7

Coach Hennessey only hit two other balls to me. I caught them both with no trouble, but he didn't seem too impressed.

Lobo kept yelling insults, mostly at the kids from Stumptown and the guys who dropped balls.

After everybody caught a few fly balls, we had to throw from the outfield to guys at second base, third base, and home.

I have a pretty strong arm, but I didn't volunteer to throw right away. I was getting shakier, and the reason was Lobo. Nerves and anger are a real bad combination when you're playing ball. So I held back till last, which probably wasn't a great idea. Lobo was yelling insults after all the bad throws. That made me even more nervous about taking my turn.

Finally everybody had thrown but me. "This oughta be good," Lobo called when I put on the glove.

I smacked the ball into my glove, pretending I was smacking it into Lobo's face. I threw to Bob Matthews on second. The ball zoomed right in, just perfect. But I threw high to third, and the throw to home went left a little. The kid squatting with the catcher's mitt couldn't reach it and he toppled over.

Lobo laughed real loud. "Hey, Stumptown!" he yelled. "My little *sister* throws better than you!"

I swear I could've knocked his head off. My nerves were shot. The tryout wasn't even over, but my dream of playing for the Wildcats had disappeared like smoke on a breeze.

The rest of the tryout didn't get any better. Coach asked us what position we wanted to play. I said "pitcher" in a low voice so Lobo wouldn't hear. But Coach Hennessey didn't let me pitch more than three balls. They weren't great pitches, I guess. The rest of the afternoon was a blur.

At the end of the tryout, Coach Hennessey read off the names of the guys who'd made the team. I didn't make it. Shame heated up and bubbled in my chest. I blinked hard, looking at the ground. I was scared that little-kid tears would work their way out of my eyes and down my face.

Will made the team. I tried to make room in my head for some happiness about that. I'd wanted him to make the team as much as I'd wanted to get picked. But there was so much embarrassment crowding into my brain right then, there wasn't much room for anything else. I shook Will's hand, and his eyes had a guilty look. I think he was feeling bad for feeling good when I didn't make the team with him.

"Hey, Will, you did good," I said. "Even with Lobo yelling out there. I guess I couldn't block him out like you told me."

Will thumped me on the back, but I turned away toward home. I rounded the backstop.

"The big kid didn't give you much of a break, huh?"

The voice was big and deep. I looked up and saw the colored man watching me. He was still sitting on the bleacher.

The sun was in my face, so I had to squint at him. "Yeah, that's Brad Lobo. He's pretty mean."

"What'd he call you? Stumptown? That your name?"

I looked at the grass. "No. Stumptown's what they call a part of Holden down by the river. That's where I live." I looked up at him. "It's a nice place."

The guy nodded. "I bet it is," he said.

I started walking again.

"Don't feel too bad about the tryout," he said, and I stopped. "You just need to practice catching and learning how to control the ball."

I squinted at him some more. He wasn't as big as his voice sounded, but he looked real strong. Maybe even as strong as Coach Hennessey. "Yeah, I guess," I said.

"I've, uh, played some ball myself." He watched me a second and it looked like his mind was working on something. Then he said, "That pitch that went left? If you throw the ball across the seams, you'll have better control. It won't likely sink or sail, either."

The burn in my chest grew when I remembered that wild pitch.

"Want to try one?" he asked.

"A pitch, you mean? Now?" I asked.

"Sure."

I didn't want to. I wanted to go home and not think about baseball for a while.

"I don't know," I said. I looked around. Everybody

from the tryouts was leaving the park. Will was walking away with one of the other guys who'd made the team. Coach Hennessey and Lobo headed toward the parking lot, loaded down with bags of equipment. I shrugged. "I can't. I don't have a ball."

A big smile spread across the man's face, and his eyes shone. "Got me one right here," he said. He leaned over and opened the sack sitting next to him. His right arm looked hurt or something. It moved funny, kind of stiff. He used his left hand to reach inside the bag and pull out the ball and a catcher's glove.

"There you go," he said. He tossed me the ball with his left hand, then put on the glove. "Try it now. Index and third finger across the seams." He backed off a ways. "Put the ball right here." He held his glove in front of his stomach.

I didn't want to hurt his feelings. He was just trying to be nice. But I didn't feel like pitching a ball, to him or anybody else.

He kept looking at me like he really wanted me to try it. So I laid my fingers across the seams like he told me, wound up, and pitched him one. It went past his right side, about a foot away. He went to get the ball.

"Follow through, now," he said. "Don't stop in the middle of your pitch. In fact, I want to see you pick some grass after the ball leaves your hand. Move your arm all the way down to the ground in one motion."

I frowned. "Pick some *grass?*"

"Yeah. Pick me a handful." He tossed the ball back to me with his good arm.

He said he'd played some ball, but it must have been some weird kind of baseball. I've never heard of a pitcher picking grass at the end of a pitch.

I didn't want to argue with him, though, because he was just trying to help. So I shrugged. "Okay."

"Right here." He held the glove in front of his stomach again.

This time, I put my fingers over the seams, wound up, and threw right at his stomach. In the same motion, my hand reached down and pulled up the grass like he told me. The ball went right to him.

He laughed. "What'd I tell you? Perfect."

I put my hands on my hips. "I'll be darned, it worked."

He just stood there and smiled.

"What's your name, anyway?" I asked him.

"Luther Peale," he said.

"Well, I'm Charlie Nebraska," I said, "and I sure do wish I'd met you a week ago."

Chapter Two

Luther's forehead was beaded with sweat. He wiped his face with the crook of his arm.

"Well, you keep practicin', Charlie," he told me. "You remember to follow through on your pitches and you'll be playin' like a pro before you know it."

"Thanks," I said.

He opened his mouth to say something else, but stopped and rubbed a hand over the stubble on his face. He looked away and back at me and finally said, "You know of anybody needin' a man to work?"

I shrugged. "No, sorry."

He nodded. "Well, I better get going." He hoisted his bag over his shoulder. "See you, Charlie." He started walking toward the road along the side of the park.

"Hey, Luther?" I called. He turned back. "My mom might know of someone wanting to hire a man. You want to ask her? She's probably home by now."

He looked like he was thinking about it. Then he nodded. "All right. I'd be much obliged."

"My house is this way." I nodded in that direction.

We headed through the park and down the sidewalk. A car drove past and the people in the back pasted their faces onto the window glass, staring at Luther. I guess I wasn't the only person surprised to see a colored man in Holden. I was kind of embarrassed for Luther, and I hoped he didn't see them. If he did, he didn't let on.

"That sure is a big sack," I said. Up close now, I could see it was made of a couple of gunnysacks sewn together. I was wondering what he was lugging in it, but it seemed kind of rude to ask. I was hoping he'd tell me.

"Just got into town last night," Luther said. "Haven't found a place to stay yet."

"Where'd you stay last night?" I asked him.

"Oh, I built a camp south of town on the river. Fixed me a lean-to and caught a catfish for supper. You got pretty good catfish in that river."

We walked along in silence while I chewed on what he'd just told me. Why didn't he just get a room somewhere instead of camping out? Maybe he didn't have the money.

I looked over at his big sack. Maybe he used it because he had too much stuff and it wouldn't all fit into a suitcase. But the sack didn't look too heavy.

I wanted to ask him where he came from and why he was here in Holden. But I didn't want be nosy, so I kept still.

We walked some more, crossed the railroad tracks,

and headed into my neighborhood. The houses here are pretty small, with just one floor and four or five rooms.

"This is Stumptown," I said. "My house is about three more blocks, down by the river."

"Interesting name, Stumptown," Luther said.

"Yeah. I guess a long time ago when people came up the river, they stopped in Holden and cut down trees for houses. They moved on with the wood and left the stumps. So when my neighborhood was built, the stumps had to be pulled out little by little, and everybody started calling the place Stumptown."

"Makes sense," Luther said.

A few more minutes went by, and then I pointed to my house on the corner. It's one floor and white. Dad used to keep the grass mowed, but since he's gone, it's been my job. It looked pretty good. Especially with the flowers blooming and the maple in the front filled out with leaves. "That's where I live," I said.

"Looks nice," Luther said.

We walked up the gravel drive and over the grass to the front stoop. I opened the screen and the hinges squealed. The big door inside was standing open.

"I can wait out here," Luther said, backing off a ways.

"How come?" I asked. "Mom works downtown, but she's always home by now. Come on in and meet her."

Luther smiled and set down his sack. "Oh, I'll just stay here and enjoy the sunshine."

I shrugged. "Okay. I'll go get us some lemonade and have her come out."

"That'll be fine," he said.

I went inside. The living room smelled of lemon oil, and the doily over the back of the davenport was straightened, so I knew Mom had done her usual Monday tidying up after work. I went to the kitchen, opened the Frigidaire, and pulled open the freezer compartment. When I took out the metal ice cube trays, my fingers stuck a little on them. I pulled up the lever, and the ice squeaked and crunched as it came loose. I filled a couple of glasses with ice and poured the lemonade from the pitcher in the Frigidaire.

Mom came in the kitchen door from the backyard, brushing a strand of dark hair out of her eyes. She was wearing the old housedress she puts on after work and an apron over that. She carried a bowl of peas in their pods, picked from the garden, and a pair of scissors. On top of the peas were some daisies she'd cut from a clump that grows next to the house.

"Oh, Charlie, I didn't know you were home," she said, heading for the sink. "How'd the tryout go, hon? Did you make the team?"

"No," I said. "I got too nervous."

"Oh, honey, that's too bad," she said. "But you're a good player. You shouldn't have been nervous."

"I know, but this kid named Brad Lobo kept yelling stuff at me."

"Brad Lobo? Do I know who he is? I don't think I've heard you mention him before." The water rushed over her hands and she turned to me, frowning. "I should've gone with you. I can't believe the coach let some boy get away with making you nervous that way."

I should've known better than to tell Mom what happened. She's always hovering around, trying to keep everything perfect. I don't tell her so, but it gets on my nerves.

"Come on outside," I said to change the subject. "I met somebody, and he's real nice."

"Oh, a new friend?" She smiled. "That's nice, Charlie. But didn't you ask him in?"

"Yeah, but he said he likes the sunshine."

"Okay," Mom said, "give me a second and I'll be out." She picked up a dish towel and ran a hand through her hair. "At least let me run a comb through this mess. The humidity makes it all frizzy."

"You look fine," I said.

I took the glasses of lemonade outside. Luther was sitting under the maple tree, his big old gunnysack next to him on the ground.

"Mom'll be right out," I said, handing him a glass.

"Thank you, Charlie," he said.

He must've been awful thirsty, because he drained the glass in a few seconds. He wiped a hand across his mouth and leaned his head back against the tree trunk and closed his eyes.

"That was the best lemonade I ever had," he said, "and that's a fact."

"There's plenty more."

Mom opened the front door and came out on the stoop. She'd taken off her apron and looked like she'd fixed her hair. She stopped when she saw Luther, like she was surprised. She came out to the maple tree.

Luther got to his feet.

"Hello," Mom said.

"Mom, this is Luther Peale," I told her. "Luther, this is my mom."

Luther lifted his cap with his left hand and shook Mom's hand with his right.

"Nice to meet you, ma'am," he said. He smiled at her but then looked at the ground. "I don't shake too good. This hand isn't what it should be."

"Luther showed me some good baseball stuff after the tryouts," I said.

"Well, that was nice of you, Luther," Mom said. She smiled, but she was peering hard at him the way a scientist might look into a microscope.

"Charlie's got a good arm," Luther said, glancing up again. "He just needs a little practice. He'll come around, you wait and see."

"Mom, do you know of anybody needing a man to work?" I asked.

"Oh. Here in Holden?" Her voice sounded far away. She cleared her throat. "Well now, let's see." She put her fingers to her mouth and looked away, thinking. "I believe Mr. Landen from the egg-buying station said the other day he was looking for help. Maybe you could talk to him."

"Thanks very much, ma'am," Luther said. "I'll go see him."

My stomach growled. I remembered I'd been so nervous about the tryouts, I hadn't eaten since breakfast. "What's for supper?"

"Spaghetti," Mom said.

"Good. Mom makes great spaghetti," I told Luther. I turned back to her. "Can Luther maybe stay for supper?"

"Oh now, Charlie," Luther began. He held up a hand and took a step back. "I better be going now."

Mom paused a second. Just past her at the house next door I saw Mrs. Banks peeking around her living room drapes. She must've seen me see her, because she let go of the drapes and backed away from the window. I still felt her eyes on us, though, like she was watching us from deeper inside the room. Mrs. Banks is an old busybody. She's always watching us, but I figured she was spying on us now because Luther was a stranger. Probably because he was colored, too.

"Well," Mom said, "if you like spaghetti, Luther, you're welcome to have some with us."

"Oh, I don't know, ma'am." He looked away into the trees.

Mom blinked a couple of times. "We'd be pleased to have you." She sounded more definite now.

"Well, if you're sure it's no trouble," Luther said slowly.

"She don't mind," I told him.

"Doesn't," Mom corrected.

"She *doesn't* mind."

"That sounds good then." Luther nodded, but he still didn't look Mom full in the face. "Thank you, ma'am."

I wondered then if Luther had eaten anything since that fish last night.

"I'm gonna get Luther some more lemonade," I said.

"I'll get it," Mom said quickly and took Luther's glass from him. She cleared her throat again. "Charlie, will you come in and help me, please?"

I followed Mom back inside. In the kitchen, she said, "It was nice of Luther to talk to you about baseball." Her voice was light, but I could tell she was deliberating on something.

"Yeah," I said. "He seems real nice."

"He does seem like a nice young man." She pulled open the Frigidaire and got hold of the pitcher. "But you know you should be careful about strangers."

"I am," I said. "I wouldn't have gone anywhere with him. And I wouldn't have brought him home, but I knew you'd be here."

She set the pitcher carefully on the counter. "I'm glad you're thinking about that, hon. I'm not trying to scare you. I just want you to keep in mind how to be safe."

"Okay."

"I'm just not sure if Vern..." Her voice trailed off.

"If Vern what?" I asked.

She poured the lemonade into Luther's glass. "Well, I'm just glad he's not coming tonight." She said it so quietly, I almost didn't hear.

"Why not?"

"Oh, it doesn't matter," she said. "We'll talk about it later."

"No, let's talk about it now," I said. "What about Vern?" I could hear my voice getting louder. Just hearing that man's name was setting my teeth on edge.

"Well..." She frowned a little. "It's just that he—he doesn't like colored people very much."

"How come?"

Mom took the pitcher back to the Frigidaire. "Well, some people are just that way. And there's no point getting him upset."

I didn't care if Vern was upset. "Why do you have to see him, anyway?" I asked her. "He's nothing like Dad. Vern couldn't be a war hero if you jammed the enemy's guns and told him exactly what to do."

"Nobody's like your dad," Mom said. "And you remember that. It's just that I...get lonely sometimes." She looked at me close for a second or two. "Being your mom is easy, sweetheart, but I'm not very good at being a dad, too. It'd be nice to have some help with that." I started to open my mouth, and she rushed on. "I don't mean for anyone to take your dad's place, honey. But it would be wonderful if you had someone to do father-son things with."

"I don't want to do father-son things with Vern."

"Now Charlie, Vern's a good man in a lot of ways. He can be very thoughtful. And he has a good, steady job."

"I still don't like him."

Mom sighed. "Charlie, Vern cares about you, you know. So don't say anything against him. Now, you go on out with Luther, and I'll call you when supper's ready."

I felt like arguing some more, but Luther was waiting for me. I took him the lemonade, and we sat under the tree.

"You sure your mama don't mind if I stay for supper?" Luther asked. He wrapped his big hands around the cold glass.

"No, she wants you to stay," I said.

"She's a nice lady."

"Yeah." I blew out, puffing out my cheeks. "I just wish she'd get rid of Vern Jardine."

"Who's that?" Luther took a drink of the lemonade.

"He's her friend. He travels around and sells brushes and vacuum cleaners. When he's in town, he comes around at suppertime, and Mom invites him to eat."

"He nice to you?"

I thought about that. "Well…he acts friendly, I guess. But you ever look into somebody's eyes and know that behind their eyes, they're different than they want you to think?"

Luther kept his eyes steady on me. "Yes, I do."

"Well, that's Vern," I said.

Luther and I didn't talk a lot after that. We sat on the grass with the breeze brushing against our faces and worked on our lemonade. I couldn't see Mrs. Banks at the window, but I figured she was still there. I felt like walking right up on her porch, knocking on the door, and saying, "What's the matter? Ain't you never seen a colored man before?" She probably didn't like colored people either. Vern Jardine should take her out instead of Mom. They'd make a good pair.

Petey Wilder, who lives about a block away, came galloping along the street wearing his cowboy hat. He's five years old, and I've never once seen him without that hat. He must think it makes him look like Hopalong Cassidy or something. He took out his pop-gun, pointed it at a robin, and made the sound of a gun blasting away. The cork flew out of the gun and he nodded, looking pleased with himself. Then he looked over at us. He squinted hard at Luther and grabbed his cowboy hat like the wind just came up.

"Hey!" he hollered. The cork from his gun was swinging back and forth in front of his knees.

"Hey, Petey," I said. I didn't know what he was about to say, but I guessed it wasn't going to be polite.

He ran over to the edge of the yard and stared at Luther. "How come he's brown?" he asked.

I couldn't think of what to say. Poor Luther must have felt like an animal in the zoo with everybody staring.

I frowned and said in a loud voice, "Petey, why don't you go on home?"

"That's okay," Luther murmured. "He didn't mean anything bad."

Petey walked into the yard and stopped. He was still staring at Luther, and he scratched his cheek. "How come he's all brown, Charlie?" he asked again.

"Some people just are," I said.

"Oh." He stared a couple more seconds. Then he nodded and galloped off again up the street.

I didn't know what to say to Luther, so I said, "Sorry."

Luther closed his eyes and held the lemonade glass up to his face, feeling the cold. "It's all right. I guess you don't have many colored people living here."

"No," I said. "We don't have any."

I wondered about that. Why didn't Holden have colored people? The town had a population of more than two thousand, but even with that many people, we didn't have a lot of things. One drive-in movie but no indoor theater. One bookstore. One dime store. Two markets and one elementary school. The high school kids were bused into Mt. Vernon. If we wanted clothes other than Sears & Roebuck, we usually drove to Cedar Rapids.

A sign on the highway coming into town says "Welcome to Holden: Population 2,100. The Town of Flowers." Somebody wrote BLOOMING IDIOTS on it in big letters, which made people really mad. The mayor ordered the sign to be repainted and offered a ten-dollar reward for anybody who would tell who did the vandalism. Nobody's spoke up yet. So anyway, I guess not everybody thinks highly of Holden.

Mom called us in to supper after a while. Luther took off his baseball cap when he came inside. The kitchen smelled like tomatoes and spices.

The kitchen table is small, and I hate being so close and bumping knees when Vern's over. But with Luther sitting there, it felt kind of cozy. The oilcloth on the table was clean, and the daisies were standing in water in a canning jar on the middle of the table.

We sat down, and Mom and I reached for food: spaghetti with tomato sauce and meatballs, bread, and green peas. We took some and passed the bowls to Luther.

"I can take you down to the egg-buying station tomorrow," I told Luther. "Mr. Landen's nice."

Luther looked at Mom, and she didn't say I couldn't, so he said, "Thank you, Charlie. I'd appreciate that."

I liked the idea that Luther might settle down around here. Maybe he'd give me some more pointers about baseball, and maybe sometime he could show me how he built his lean-to.

It was good having him here.

But that good feeling didn't last long. Because right then, Vern Jardine walked through the front door.

Chapter Three

Hello! Mary?" Vern called from the living room.

Mom froze a second. Then she cleared her throat. "In the kitchen, Vern."

I whispered to Mom, "Why don't he knock?" and she waved at me to be quiet.

Footsteps clomped across the wood floor in the living room. "Thought I'd surprise you. I didn't think I'd get here tonight, but I sold all the—"

Vern stopped in the kitchen doorway and his smile faded. He was wearing the wrinkly tan suit he wore a lot, and his hair was messed up. He stared at Luther.

Mom stood up and her hand went up to her collar. "Oh—Vern, this is a friend of Charlie's," she said. "Luther—what did you say your last name is?"

"Peale, ma'am," Luther said. He looked back and forth between Mom and Vern.

Mom was nervous. Her hands fluttered around her neck and hair like a couple of butterflies. "Yes, that's right, Luther Peale."

I realized that I was feeling jittery, too, and it made me mad. What was I nervous about? So what if Vern didn't like colored people? This wasn't his house.

Mom's smile at Vern was crooked. "And Luther taught Charlie some things about baseball today."

Vern stared at Luther, his jaw set hard. "Can I talk to you privately, Mary?" he asked.

"Sure." Mom hurried after him into the living room. The front screen door banged shut, but we could hear them talking fast and whispery clear out on the front stoop.

Why did Vern have to show up now, just when we were all having a good time?

I tried to drown out the sounds by talking, and the words were flying fast out of my mouth.

"So I'll take you to the egg-buying place tomorrow," I told Luther. "It's not very far from here. Maybe six blocks or eight blocks away, so we'll just walk down there—"

"I better be goin', Charlie," he said quietly. He stood up and picked up his cap that he'd put on the table next to him.

"No, Luther, don't go."

Vern's voice was getting louder, and we could hear what he was saying to Mom. "You asked him to sit right down and *eat* with you?"

"Vern, he's Charlie's friend," Mom said.

"I'm just concerned about you and the boy," Vern said. "You know that."

Luther picked up his bag near the table. "You tell your mama I'm much obliged for the spaghetti."

"But you hardly ate any!" I said, jumping up from the table. "Luther, don't go. I hate Vern."

The gears in my brain were whirring around like crazy, and my head was pounding with the banging of my heart.

"It was good to meet you, Charlie," he said. "I'll see you." Then he was gone out the door.

"Luther!" I yelled. "Come back!"

But Luther was already walking across the grass and into Mrs. Banks's yard near the shed at the back. I ran out the door and followed him.

Mom yelled from the back door. "Charlie! Where're you going?"

"I'm going to talk to Luther!" I yelled at her.

"No, Charlie!" she hollered. She came running and caught up with me in the yard behind ours. She took my arm, but I shook her off. I was so filled up with anger I couldn't hardly talk.

I saw Mrs. Banks standing at her back screen door, but I didn't care.

"I hate Vern!" I yelled. "I hate him!"

A look of misery came into Mom's eyes. "Charlie, you come back now. Vern left."

"What about Luther?" I looked back over my shoulder and saw that he was nearly a half block away.

"Honey, Luther's a grown man," Mom said. She glanced over at Mrs. Banks's back door and lowered her voice way down. "He can take care of himself. Maybe Mr. Landen will give him that job at the egg-buying station. Come on, Charlie. Let's go in the house now." She glanced over again at Mrs. Banks's house.

"Mom, he's hungry."

"Lower your voice," Mom murmured, giving me a hard look, "and go inside."

She nudged me and nodded toward our back door.

I walked inside with her. I kept my voice low. "Mom, I don't think he's had any food since he caught a fish in the river last night. We gotta help him." I saw her eyes go soft, so I kept on. "When Vern was talking about him, Luther heard him, and you shoulda seen his face."

"Ohhh." Mom looked miserable again. She put a hand to her mouth. "I'm so sorry."

"We can take him some spaghetti," I said. "I'm pretty sure I can find him."

"Oh, Charlie..."

"Please, Mom? He don't know anybody in Holden, and he don't have a job yet."

It was a second before she took a deep breath and said, "Okay. Put some spaghetti in a bowl and cover it with tin foil. The rest can go in the Frigidaire. I'll get the keys and back out the car."

"Thanks, Mom."

"And get a fork and a napkin from the drawer."

"Okay."

In a few minutes we were in the old Chevy heading out of Stumptown. I had the bowl of spaghetti on my lap and a fork and napkin in my hand.

"He said he was staying down by the river," I said. "He set up camp down there."

"Set up camp?" A frown worked onto her face. She slowed the car, then stopped.

"What?" I said.

"Oh, honey," she said. "I don't think this is a good idea." She turned to face me. "You mean he's a drifter?"

"No, he came here looking for work," I said, talking fast. "I told you! He's just camping out till he gets a job. But he's hungry, and he heard what Vern said, so he left before he had a chance to eat. Please, Mom."

I could see she was softening again. She nodded. "Okay, we'll take him the spaghetti. And that's that."

She started driving again.

I wasn't sure exactly what Mom meant by "that's that," but at least we were going to get Luther some food tonight.

"He said he caught a catfish last night," I told her. "Said it was pretty good. But I bet he'll be glad to get the spaghetti."

We drove along the edge of downtown and headed toward the river. We passed a big warehouse, a tavern, and the corner market.

"Charlie," Mom said, "I don't want you to think bad things about Vern. He's—"

"I don't want to talk about him," I said. "I hate him."

"You shouldn't say that," Mom said. "It's not right to hate a person."

"Well, tell Vern not to hate colored people then."

"Charlie, we need to talk." She was saying the words slow and careful, and she slowed the car down to a crawl. "Vern and I might be getting married, you know."

"What?" I said. "How can you even *like* him?"

"Honey, he helped me feel better after your dad died," Mom said. "I still miss your dad something terrible—you know that—but sometimes when I'm with Vern, I can forget for a few minutes. Just a few minutes." She turned a corner. "It's hard being alone."

I didn't see what was so hard about it. And she wasn't alone. Mom and I were doing fine. She had the job at Woolworth's, and I helped out a lot and did some of the jobs around the house that Dad would've done if he was here. I mowed the lawn and shoveled the snow, dried the dishes every night, and I helped Mom lift heavy things when she needed it.

"Has he asked you to marry him?" I said.

"Well, no, not yet." Mom was still driving real slow. "I just have a feeling." She frowned. "Unless..." Her voice trailed off.

I knew what she was thinking. "I hope Vern's so mad, he never comes back," I said. "I don't want him living in our house."

"Well, if we get married, Charlie, we'd probably move out of Stumptown into a nicer place."

"We've got a nice place," I said.

It scared me to think about moving. Sometimes I'm sure I'll look up one day and see Dad walk through the front door. I mean, what if he wasn't really killed in Korea and they sent somebody else's body home by mistake? Everyone told Mom not to open the coffin, and she didn't. What if he's alive in a prison in North Korea? The war has to end someday, and then he could come home.

Sometimes I believe that, and other times I don't know.

But what if it really *did* happen that way, and Dad came home and someone else was living in our house? How would he find us?

I couldn't let that happen.

Mom turned onto a street that would take us along the Red Cedar River to our left. The Red Cedar's a pretty big river, and deep, too. I've been swimming in it, but I'd never tell Mom. She'd scream if she knew. Will told me that people drown in the river every couple of years. Last year, it was a guy from over at the high school. He was goofing off with friends and jumped off the Rock Island railroad bridge and never came up again. His body washed up downriver two days later.

As we drove, I wondered if we might pass Luther's camp and not see it. Trees and brush grow right up to the water's edge in most places. Luther could've built a camp in the brush and we'd never spot it driving by in the car.

But then we came even to where the clearing is. You couldn't see it from where we were, because the road backs away a little and the ground slopes down.

"Stop the car," I said.

"You see him?" Mom asked, staring hard at the woods across the street.

"No, but I bet he's down there," I said. "Park right here, at the side of the road."

Mom stopped the car and looked at the dense trees growing on the slope that dipped out of sight. "You're not walking through that timber," she said. "There's bound to be lots of ticks in the grass. They'll run right up your legs."

"Mom, Luther may be down there," I said, pushing open the car door. "Besides, the timber's not deep. There're just a few trees."

She frowned. "Well, let's see."

"Come on," I said. I brought the bowl of spaghetti, the fork, and the napkin.

She crossed the street behind me, and I led her to the top of the slope.

"See?" I said. "It's not so steep. And there's a path down to the river right here."

"Okay," Mom said. "But be careful, Charlie. You want me to hold that dish of spaghetti?"

"No, I've got it," I said.

I led her along the path as it wound down the slope. The sunlight was thinner now as the day eased into evening, and the trees sieved what was left of it into tiny flecks of gold that splashed over the green. Our footsteps tromped on the soft ground, crunching leaves and twigs.

At the bottom we came to the clearing. I saw Luther's catfish line first. It was tied to a stick about two feet tall that was jammed into the sandy ground next to the river. The line stretched out into the water and looked pretty limp, so there wasn't a fish on the other end.

Then I saw the lean-to built with brush. It stood up against some bushes, making a great shelter for someone underneath. It wouldn't have kept all the rain out, but maybe it'd keep off a few sprinkles if they weren't coming down too hard.

A circle of rocks made a place for a campfire. Off to the side, a wire about a hundred feet long was tied between two trees. I figured Luther was using that to hang out his clothes after he washed them in the river.

It was a great camp.

"Luther's staying here?" Mom said in a low voice. "Oh, Charlie. He seems like a nice man, but maybe we should—"

"Luther?" I called out, ignoring her. "It's Charlie. Me and Mom came to see you."

Luther's head popped out from the lean-to. "Charlie?" he asked.

I held up the dish in my hands. "We brought you some spaghetti 'cause you didn't get to eat."

Luther stepped out of the lean-to, looking surprised. "What?" he said.

"We didn't want you to be hungry," I said.

Luther walked toward us slowly. "Oh, you didn't have to do that," he said in a shy kind of voice.

I went to him and handed him the dish and fork. He nodded. "Well, that's real nice of you." He smiled a little at Mom. "Mrs. Nebraska, you do make good spaghetti."

Mom nodded back. I wanted her to say thank you to his compliment, but she didn't. She kept staring at the lean-to. Then she'd look over at Luther and back at the lean-to. Something was working hard in her head, like maybe worrying that Luther was an escaped criminal or something. I kept searching through my mind for the right thing to say. But it seemed like there was so much noise going on in her mind, she wouldn't hear me, anyway.

Luther was watching Mom, too. "Come and sit down," he said. He waved at a fallen log. "It's not fancy, but it's pretty comfortable."

"Thanks." I sat on the log. "You made a great camp."

"Thank you, Charlie." He looked at Mom, who was still standing stiff next to the circle of campfire rocks. "Mrs. Nebraska," he said in a soft voice, "I'll only be stayin' at this camp till I get a job and can get me a room."

35

"Come on," I said to Mom. "Sit down." I patted the log next to me.

Mom stepped carefully over the rough ground. "Tell me, um, Luther..." She brushed off the log and sat down. "What brings you here to Holden?"

He looked down at the spaghetti dish in his hands. "Oh, I was ready for a change, I guess you could say."

"Go ahead and eat," I told him.

Luther smiled. "Thank you," he said. He nodded at Mom. "Ma'am."

He sat down on a tree stump and took the foil off the dish. He scooped up spaghetti with the fork and crammed it into his mouth. The noodles, covered with red sauce, dangled from his lips. With a combination of sucking them in and using his fork, he got it all into his mouth.

He wiped his lips with the back of his hand.

"Charlie," Mom said, "did you bring Luther the napkin?"

"Oh, I forgot." I still had it rolled up in my hand. I got up and gave it to Luther and stood next to him, watching him eat.

"I swear, I'm hungry enough to eat the south end of a northbound polecat," he said between bites.

The edges of Mom's mouth twitched up into an almost-smile. "Where do you come from, Luther?" she asked.

"Tennessee, ma'am," he said.

"You must be about—what?—twenty-four years old?"

"Twenty-five, ma'am."

"And what work did you do in Tennessee?" she asked.

I wished she wouldn't ask him so many questions, especially while he was trying to eat.

Luther swallowed the mouthful and said, "I played baseball, ma'am."

"No," Mom said. "I mean, how did you earn your living?"

"Baseball, ma'am. I played with the Memphis Mockingbirds."

Mom stared at him, blinking, and Luther added, "They're a team with the Negro League."

"Wow. You're a professional baseball player?" I asked.

I thought of the advice he gave me after tryouts and suddenly realized I'd been coached by a genuine pro. "Did you ever meet Jackie Robinson?"

"I sure did, Charlie," Luther said. "Back in forty-five. Jackie's a champion, and that's a fact. I'll tell you about him someday."

"Why did you stop playing?" Mom asked.

I wanted to know, too, but it was embarrassing the way she asked, like maybe she thought he got kicked off the team or something.

"I hurt my arm, ma'am," he said. "Couldn't play no more."

Mom finally stopped asking questions and we let Luther eat. He sure was hungry. It only took him about two minutes to eat it all. When he was finished, he went to the river and washed the dish and fork.

"Thank you for bringing the spaghetti, ma'am," Luther said when he came back. "It was real good." He handed the dish, fork, and napkin to Mom.

"This is a great camp, Luther," I said, looking around. I ran for the lean-to.

"Don't go in there, Charlie..." Luther said, coming after me.

But I was already there and stepped inside. Luther's sack was on the ground. An open bottle sat on a tree stump in the middle. It was nearly full. I stared at it. It looked like the whiskey that my grand-dad drank on special occasions.

It was weird that Luther didn't have food, but he had whiskey. I once saw Eileen's dad drunk, and later Mom explained he had trouble with drinking. Luther looked okay, though, not like Eileen's dad.

But Mom didn't drink at all, and if she saw that whiskey bottle of Luther's, she wouldn't like it.

I didn't want to mess with Luther's things, but even more, I didn't want Mom to tell me I couldn't see him again. So I picked up the bottle and set it down behind the stump.

"Charlie?" Luther stood in the opening to the lean-to. "I think your mama's ready to go home."

I came out of the lean-to and Luther gave me a little nod. I'm not sure, but I think he was thanking me for putting the bottle out of sight.

"I'll come by tomorrow and take you to the egg-buying place," I said.

"Um, Luther, why don't you come to our house and meet Charlie?" Mom said quickly. "Then you both can walk to see Mr. Landen."

I could tell Mom didn't want me coming back here. But Luther's camp was real inviting, and I wanted to come back again as soon as I could. Just before he found out he had to go into the Army, Dad said he'd take me camping. But we never got to do it.

So I was already planning how I could come back here.

I do what Mom tells me most of the time. But once in a while I do something different. Like I said, it's not very often.

Just often enough so I don't go completely crazy.

Chapter Four

Luther knocked on our door about nine o'clock the next morning.

"Hi," I said, opening the screen door. Its rusty hinges creaked like a complaining cat. "Come on in. I was just having breakfast. You want some?"

Luther didn't move. "Um, Charlie..."

"Yeah?"

He looked around. "Is that fella here?" he asked quietly.

"Nah, luckily," I said. "Vern usually comes over after work."

Luther nodded and came inside. Mom was in her bedroom getting ready for work. She'd just turned up the radio in the living room so she could hear Nat King Cole sing a song about some girl named Mona Lisa. It was her favorite song.

I led Luther into the kitchen.

"You want some oatmeal?" I asked. "Or toast?" I pointed to our toaster that was so shiny you could see your face in it. Our old toaster broke last winter, so we saved enough S&H Green Stamps to get a new one last month.

"Your mama's going to think I eat all my meals here," Luther said. He didn't move to sit down.

"She made some extra for you, in case you wanted it," I told him. It was sort of a lie, but I figured Luther wouldn't eat unless he thought it was okay with Mom. And I knew she wouldn't mind.

Luther smiled. "Your mama's a special lady, and that's a fact," he said.

I dished him up most of the oatmeal from the pan on the stove and put the rest in my bowl. Then I gave him the sugar bowl and the milk bottle from the Frigidaire. We ate without talking much, but that was okay.

Mom came to the kitchen doorway, smoothing her hair with both hands. "Hello, Luther. Charlie taking you to Landen's this morning?"

"Yes, ma'am."

"Well, that's good. Kiss and a hug, Charlie," she said, leaning down.

I pointed one side of my face at her, so she could kiss it, and I let her hug me, but I didn't hug back. Boys as old as me don't do that kind of stuff in front of other people. It's embarrassing.

"Oh, hon," Mom said. "Mrs. Crawford called yesterday. A book that I reserved came in. So could you go to the library sometime today and pick it up?"

"Okay."

"Thanks, sweetie." She kissed me again. "Now you be good, and call me if you need anything."

I rolled my eyes at Luther, and he tried not to smile.

Mom walks to her job at Woolworth's on nice days to save on gas. She said good-bye and went out the front door.

"I sure do wish she'd quit babying me," I said to Luther.

"I wish my mama was still alive to baby me," he said.

"What happened to her?" I asked.

"Pneumonia," Luther said. "She was a good woman."

After the Army told us that Dad died, I thought about what would happen if Mom died. I'd be an orphan. I guess I'd have to go live with my Aunt Glenda and Uncle Burt in the country near Keokuk. That would be real bad because Aunt Glenda can't cook for nothing, and Uncle Burt spends all his free time sitting on the porch, chewing. I don't see how he can stand it. His teeth are brown and his breath so bad, I lose my appetite around him. Between her bad cooking and his chewing tobacco, I figure I'd be close to starvation in a month.

Besides, if my mom died, I'd feel awful lonely. Sometimes I can't hardly stand it that my Dad's not here anymore. Me and him played catch every night of the summer before he left for the war. That was the best summer I ever had. A familiar hollow space opened up in my chest when I thought about Dad. I didn't want to go into that dark place now. So I said, "Ready to go?"

"Ready," Luther answered.

We walked toward the egg-buying station downtown. It seemed like on every street people turned to stare at us. Luther must have noticed it, too.

When we got to the corner of Main and Ash, a truck came up the street with two men in it. The driver slowed as they got near. His window was open, and his elbow stuck out. He gave Luther a mean look and said, "What're you doin' here, boy? You don't belong here."

Luther looked at the ground. "Just keep walkin'," he mumbled so soft I almost didn't hear. "If there's any trouble, you keep movin'."

I looked up at Luther and back at the truck.

"Don't look at 'em, Charlie," he said, still real soft.

Luther seemed calm, but his eyes had a sharp, focused look. My body felt charged with electricity. I was ready to put up my fists or run, depending on what Luther and those men did.

The truck rolled on by, though, and I heaved out a big breath.

"They might be back," Luther said.

"Come on." I touched his arm. "Let's go down the alley. It's faster, anyway."

I hurried down the alley with Luther following. I glanced back over my shoulder at him. "This happen to you in other towns?"

"Many times," he said. A second later, he repeated in a tired voice, "Many times."

It hardly seemed possible that there were that many people around who didn't like colored folks they hadn't even met yet. It didn't make sense to me. I couldn't see anything about Luther that was different from anyone else, except his skin was darker. In the summer, people lie around in the sun trying to make their skin tan. In Luther's case, he just started out a darker shade.

A minute later we were at Landen's. It's a small place between a tavern and the railroad tracks.

I opened the screen door and we walked in. The wax on the wood floor was polished so glossy, I could see the gleam of the overhead light reflected in it. The floor creaked under our shoes as we crossed it. Mr. Landen was sitting at a small desk behind the counter. He looked up.

"Hi, Mr. Landen," I said.

I'd met him a bunch of times. He helps out with the Fourth of July fireworks in the park every year, and I've seen him at a few Wildcats games. My dad seemed to like him, so I figured he'd be nice to Luther.

I was surprised how he looked when he came over. Not mean, but he didn't smile. "Hello. It's Charlie, right?" he said. "Bill Nebraska's boy?"

"Yes, sir," I answered. I turned to Luther. "This is Luther Peale. He's looking for a job, and Mom said you need help."

"Well, yes, I do," Mr. Landen said. He examined Luther, his head tipped back, squinting through the lower part of his thick glasses. Then he stuck out his hand. "Hello, Luther."

Luther said hello and shook the man's hand.

"You ever candle eggs?" Mr. Landen asked, still squinting.

"Yes, sir," Luther said. "My daddy works a farm in Tennessee, and I was in charge of the hatchery and chickens."

"That right?"

"Yes, sir," Luther said. "I turned the eggs under the lamps every day. Put X's and O's on 'em so I could keep track of which ones I'd turned. I fed the chickens, candled the eggs so we wouldn't go sellin' the bad ones, and I helped my mama butcher the chickens we ate."

Mr. Landen folded his arms across his chest and nodded. "What kind of chickens you raise on your farm?"

"At first we had leghorns 'cause they lay so many eggs," Luther said. "But they're skinny and light, and they kept flyin' over the fence. So we got Plymouth Rock and White Rock hens. They have better meat for eatin', anyway."

Mr. Landen's face relaxed into a smile. "Well, you know your chickens. All right, Luther," he said. "I think you'll do fine."

I laughed and thumped Luther on the arm. He put his other hand over that right arm.

"I gotta tell you, Mr. Landen," Luther said. "I got a bad arm here. I can lift with it, but nothing too heavy, and only so high." He lifted a shaky right arm as high as his chest.

"Well, you wouldn't have to do the overhead lifting," Mr. Landen said. "There isn't much of that anyway. I'll start you out and see how it goes."

"Thank you, sir," Luther said.

"You'll be working Monday through Friday, nine to five. Pay is minimum wage: seventy-five cents an hour."

"Sounds fine," Luther said.

"When can you start?"

"I'm ready," Luther told him. "Whenever you need me."

"How about right now?" Mr. Landen asked. "I'm having a hard time keeping up."

"Right now's fine," Luther said, nodding.

I was a little disappointed, because I'd been hoping we could walk over to Luther's camp. But I was glad he got the job.

He turned to me. "Thanks for bringing me here, Charlie," he said. "I'll see you soon. I want to thank your mama for letting me know about the job."

"How about tonight?" I asked. Then I remembered that Mom had said Vern was coming by for supper. "Oh, I guess tonight isn't good."

Luther nodded. "Some other time, then."

"Okay," I said. "See you later."

Luther turned and followed Mr. Landen behind the counter and into the back room.

I went outside and headed toward the library. It was on the other side of downtown Holden, which is only about three blocks long.

Holden's a small town except during the Sweet Corn Festival in August. Crowds come in from bigger cities, like Cedar Rapids and Mt. Vernon, and our town swells up with about twice as many people as usual. For those two days, the downtown streets are blocked to traffic. You can buy cotton candy, and ride Ferris wheels, and pay a nickel for the chance to shoot a target and win a prize. When I was about seven, Dad won a snow globe. It's a clear plastic ball that's filled with water. It has a winter scene inside, and when you shake it, these little white specks float around, and it looks like it's snowing. He gave it to me, and it's sitting on the table next to my bed.

I climbed the front steps to the Holden Carnegie Library. It's a vine-covered brick building, and I visit it about once a week in the summertime. Mom reads a lot. She says I have to read one book for every five comic books I buy at the drugstore.

I pulled open the heavy glass door and went inside.

Mrs. Crawford sat at the circulation desk reading some papers that were spread out in front of her. I stood next to the desk till she looked up.

"Oh, hi, Charlie," she said. "Are you here to pick up your mom's book?"

"Yeah," I said.

"Say, I just processed a new Heinlein book called *Between Planets*. It's upstairs in the juvenile section." She looked at me over her glasses. "It's a lot better than those comic books you're always reading."

I shrugged.

"Where do you suppose the heroes buy those blue tights they always wear while they're flying around saving people?"

She was teasing, but I said seriously, "I have a lot of really good comic books. But the Heinlein books are good, too."

Mrs. Crawford's eyebrows went up. "Very diplomatic, Charlie," she said. "Maybe you'll work for the government someday."

That didn't sound very interesting, but I shrugged again. "Maybe. I'll go up and get the new book."

I took the stairs two at a time to the second floor.

I like the upstairs part of the library. It's really a loft, and you can look down over the railing onto the library's main floor and circulation desk. It's pretty quiet, and on slow days, I can be the only person up there for an hour or more. I sit in this big, soft chair near the door to the stairs and hang one leg over the armrest and read while Mom talks to Mrs. Crawford or looks for books on the main floor. When it's time to go, Mom clears her throat. I look down at her, she waves, and I meet her downstairs.

The juvenile section is in some stacks on the right

side. I followed along the shelves and found *Between Planets* by Robert Heinlein right away, at the end of the G–J stack. I pulled it off the shelf and read the description on the cover. It looked pretty good.

A door in the back wall opened, and Mr. Billett came out. He was lugging a big box.

"Hey, Mr. Billett," I said. "Need some help?" I grabbed the door and held it open.

Mr. Billet works at the library. He keeps it clean and sometimes shelves books and stuff.

I peeked through the doorway behind him. There was a small, messy room with two desks and a table piled with stuff.

"Thanks, Charlie," he said. "Want to help me get this downstairs? It's heavier than I thought." He huffed out a heavy breath. "Sure would be nice if we could get an elevator installed here."

"Yeah," I said. "Or we could make a pulley thing and lower the box over the railing from the edge of the loft."

He laughed. "Okay, Charlie, if you make the pulley thing, I'll use it."

I tossed the Heinlein book on top of the box and grabbed hold of it. We balanced the box between us.

"You got books in there?" I asked.

"Yep. New ones, ready to go on the shelves."

We edged to the stairs and took them real slow to the bottom. We crossed the floor and set the box on the circulation desk.

"Oh, Charlie," Mrs. Crawford said, looking up from her desk, "I hear you have a birthday coming up."

"On the sixteenth," I said, surprised. "Did Mom tell you that?"

She got a look on her face then that made me think she remembered she wasn't supposed to say nothing.

Mrs. Crawford shrugged. "She might have."

I smiled because I bet Mom told her about my present. I hadn't hinted about anything I wanted, so I couldn't guess what it was.

"Thanks for the help, Charlie," Mr. Billet said. "If I don't see you before the sixteenth, have a happy birthday."

"Thanks."

I checked out my book and Mom's and left the library. It was still pretty early, so I didn't want to go home yet. Maybe somebody was at the park playing ball.

I walked the five blocks to Scott Park. Johnny O'Toole and Brian Malone were there, along with Eileen McNally. Me and Will usually play here with them, too, but Will wasn't here this time. Maybe he'd come later.

The memory of tryouts yesterday was a fresh attack in my head. I didn't want my chest to heat up again, so I pushed the tryouts out of my thoughts and hurried toward the baseball diamond.

Johnny, Brian, and Eileen were all just fooling around, playing catch. It was a nice day, not so hot yet, and the sun was shining soft through the trees.

I crossed the grass toward them, and Johnny called out, "Hey, Charlie's here!"

"Charlie!" Eileen hollered.

Eileen's the only girl in a family of nine brothers, so she plays ball real good, better than most boys I know. Shortstop is her specialty, because she's fast and has a strong arm. She's got a nose for the ball, too.

Johnny came up and clapped me on the back.

"You seen Will?" I asked them.

"He came by a while ago," Johnny said. "Was goin' to play ball with some of the Wildcat guys."

"They're practicing this morning?" I was surprised. Wildcats always practice after Coach Hennessey gets off work at five.

"Naw," Johnny said, "he was just goin' to play some catch with them over at Hayes School."

"Oh." I thought about that. Will was my best friend, and he's not the kind to get stuck-up about playing with the Wildcats, even though they're the winningest team for miles. But I was surprised that he was playing with them outside of practice, and it made me feel kind of bad. He always said Johnny, Brian, Eileen, and me were the most fun to play ball with because we didn't take things so serious that we'd argue about whether a runner was safe or not. I hoped when he played with some of the other guys today, he'd see they weren't as much fun as we were.

"We should get some more kids and play workup," I

said. Workup's a way to practice so everybody gets to rotate through all the positions.

"Eileen, go call a bunch of your brothers, okay? At least get Alan, Bowie, and Casey."

The McNally kids had Irish names, and they were named in alphabetical order like hurricanes. I'm not fooling. Eileen says it wasn't on purpose at first. But after Casey was named, Mr. and Mrs. McNally realized that the first three were in alphabetical order, so they decided to keep it up. Eileen says her mom swears she's not going to have a whole alphabet full of kids.

"Okay," Eileen said. "Be right back." She grabbed her bike and rode off toward her house, which was about three blocks away.

When she came back about fifteen minutes later, five of her brothers were with her. Plus they brought four other kids they saw on the way. One was Walter Pink. He has catcher's equipment and likes that position, and we're glad to let him have it. Jim Holladay came, too. He's a good friend of Brian's. The other two were girls, Kathleen Grady and Leslie White. Kathleen and Leslie also had families with lots of brothers. They're good ballplayers. Not as good as Eileen, but pretty good.

"Okay if I play pitcher and not rotate for a while?" I asked. I wanted to practice what Luther had taught me yesterday after Wildcat tryouts.

"Okay," Johnny said. "Rest of us, 'cept Charlie and Walter, can rotate."

Everybody ran to stake out where they were playing first.

Finn, another one of the McNally kids, had brought a bat—it was cracked but taped up good—and he stood in the batter's box, ready for the pitch.

I thought about what Luther told me and laid my index and second fingers across the seams on the ball. I wound up and delivered a fastball, following through the way Luther taught me, bringing my hand all the way down to the ground. There wasn't grass to pick up, just dirt, so I touched the dirt in my follow-through.

The pitch was good. Finn smashed it to the outfield and Bowie caught it no problem.

In a workup, that means Finn takes Bowie's position in left field, and Bowie comes in to wait to bat.

"Hey, good pitch!" Johnny called out to me.

I smiled. I'd have to tell him later what Luther taught me. I wanted to tell Will, too. He could use it when he was playing for the Wildcats.

"Uh-oh," Walter said behind his catcher's mask. "Lookee who just arrived."

I turned and saw Brad Lobo and three of his baseball buddies walking right toward us through the park. I blinked and focused my eyes again, but I hadn't been seeing things.

One of the guys walking behind Lobo was Will.

"Hey, Will!" Brian called out.

Will lifted his chin but didn't say nothing. He looked real serious.

"Wanna play with us, Will?" Walter called out. His voice was high for a boy, and he was on the heavy side. Lobo smirked at him.

"No, he doesn't want to play," Lobo said in a high, girly voice, making fun of Walter.

Will didn't say anything. I knew he didn't like how Lobo was talking to Walter. Usually he stood up for guys getting picked on, but this time he stayed quiet.

"Keep playing, Charlie," Johnny said in a low voice from first base. "Ignore 'em."

Kathleen was up at bat now. Like I expected, Lobo had something to say about that.

"Whooee! The Stumptown boys play with *girls!*" Lobo hollered.

He and the other guys stopped outside the diamond, between home plate and first base. Will hung back a ways and watched.

My heart drummed in my ears. I didn't want to play bad the way I did at tryouts.

"Come on, Charlie," Johnny said. "Let's play."

I took a deep breath that was a little shaky, laid my fingers across the seams, and wound up. I threw the pitch but forgot to follow through, and the ball went left.

"Ball one!" Walter called out.

Lobo and the boys standing with him laughed. "Stumptown can't even strike out a girl!" Lobo yelled.

"Hey," Alan yelled at Lobo from third base. Alan was sixteen, four years older than him. "Cut the chatter out there!"

"Whassa matter?" Lobo yelled. "Can't concentrate 'cause we're too *loud?*"

Alan took about five steps toward Lobo, but Finn, now shortstop, rushed over and grabbed his arm.

"He's not worth it," Finn said.

"Come on, let's play," Johnny called out.

Concentrate, I told myself. *Remember what Luther said.*

This time I kept my mind clear and pitched a good one to Kathleen, right over the plate. She connected and hit a grounder up to Johnny on second base. He scooped up the ball and fired it to Brian on first. Kathleen was out.

We'd all done our jobs, so Lobo had nothing to yell about and he kept quiet. I glanced over and Will nodded to me. I figured he was saying, *Good job.*

Now Brian moved to the batter's box, Johnny moved from second to first, and Finn went from shortstop to second. Alan on third became shortstop. Kathleen went to right field, Casey went to center, Devin took Bowie's place in left field, and Bowie moved in line to bat.

Now it was Leslie's turn.

"Hey, how come you're not at home cookin' and sewin'?" Lobo called out in a high-pitched voice that was supposed to sound like a girl.

I couldn't hardly take any more. "What a creep," I muttered.

Lobo must've had hearing like Superman, because he yelled, "What? What did you say, Stumptown?"

I looked at him and he was staring right at me. My heart started hammering even harder.

"Nothin'," I mumbled.

"What? Say it again."

"I said I didn't say nothin'," I repeated.

"I think you called me a name, Stumptown," Lobo said.

He came out and stood there on the line between home and first base, his hands on his hips.

"He called you a creep, Lobo," said one of Lobo's friends. He sneered, probably thinking about what Lobo was going to do to me now. Will was watching from behind. He looked scared.

"Lobo, I wouldn't start nothin'," Alan called out. "You got three guys. We got thirteen." He obviously wasn't counting Will on Lobo's side, but he wasn't counting him on our side, either.

Lobo looked kind of startled, like he hadn't thought about that. Then he smirked and said, "Three o' yours don't count. They're girls."

"You ain't seen nothing till you seen these girls fight," Walter said behind his catcher's mask. "They're like tigers. They could tear you apart."

"That so, lardbutt?" Lobo hollered. He rushed headlong at Walter.

Walter, who'd been crouched in the catcher's position, reeled back in surprise and fear and toppled over in the dirt.

That was it for me. I'd been holding in my anger over Lobo at the tryouts. But when he went for Walter, the weakest kid in the neighborhood, I lost control and ran at him, screaming.

Lobo was unprepared. I knocked him to the ground and began whomping on him real good. He yelled real loud, grabbed my hair, and pulled hard.

I could hear all the guys running to us, shouting. Alan and Bowie hauled me off Lobo, who was still on his back on the ground, blood spurting from his nose. His buddies pulled him off the ground, and Lobo held onto his nose. The blood was pumping all over his shirt.

He lunged at me, screaming words you read on bathroom walls, but his buddies held him so he couldn't come closer.

"You better watch your back," Lobo cried, pointing at me and jabbing the air with his finger. "'Cause I'm gonna kill you, Stumptown! You hear me? I'm gonna kill you."

Chapter Five

I sat at the kitchen table and watched Vern Jardine stuff his mouth with my mom's fried chicken and mashed potatoes. His face was long and narrow, and I couldn't help thinking that he looked a little like a horse. His teeth were even kind of big. The more I thought about it, the more I wished he *was* a horse. I'd much rather my mom had a horse by that name than a boyfriend who sat across the table from me and bumped my knees. I shifted my legs to one side.

Whinny, Vern. Giddy-up.

"You've really outdone yourself, Mary," he said. He'd taken off his suit jacket and stuck his napkin in the neck of his shirt so he wouldn't mess up his front. He rubbed a corner of it over his mouth and said, "This is a great meal. Wouldn't you say so, Charlie?"

"Uh-hunh," I said.

The daisies were still standing in the canning jar on the table. It had been nice having company when Luther sat in the chair where Vern's butt was parked now. At least, it was nice until Vern showed up.

"After supper I have a surprise for you two," Vern said.

"What is it, Vern?" Mom smiled.

"I wrote another song," he said. "This one's for you, hon, and I'll sing it for you both."

Mom's smile faded a bit, and I had all I could do to keep my face straight. Vern Jardine's got the worst voice in the whole world, and when he sings, I swear if we had dogs in the neighborhood, they'd be howling under the windows.

It was amazing how a day could start out so good and end up so rotten. After I left Luther at Landen's it had all gone downhill. Everyone was excited after Lobo left the park. They slapped me on the back and said I was some kind of hero for sticking up for Walter and fighting Lobo, who had a good three inches and maybe ten or fifteen pounds on me.

But if you want to know the truth, it was just dumb luck. I knocked him off his feet is all I did.

But I kept thinking about Will and how he didn't say a word to Lobo when he was yelling stuff at us. And how he didn't move to help when Lobo attacked Walter or when I was fighting Lobo. When Lobo threatened me at the end, Will looked real upset, though. I think he was trying to tell me with his eyes that he was sorry. But he left with Lobo and those guys. Maybe he was scared, or maybe he didn't want them mad at him, but I couldn't help thinking that he wasn't as much my friend today as he was a few days ago. I thought about calling him when I got home but decided not to. He should call *me* if he wanted to talk about it.

And now Lobo had it in for me. Johnny had said, "Lobo's right, Charlie. You'd better watch your back. If he says he'll get you, he'll get you."

"Lobo didn't say he'd get me," I told him. "He said he'll *kill* me."

"That's what I meant," Johnny said. "So watch your back." Then a little smile crept across his face, and he said, "Man oh man, you shoulda seen his face when you clobbered him!"

We laughed, but to tell you the truth, I was feeling scared. I'd knocked Lobo over once, but I'd never be able to do it again. Not if he saw me coming, anyway.

Luckily I didn't have a mark on me, and Mom didn't ask about my dirty clothes. They weren't any dirtier than usual, I guess.

Now I watched Vern eating. I couldn't see what Mom liked about him, or why she'd even think of marrying him. My dad was a hero in Korea. He saved the life of another soldier. Dad was smart and could build stuff, and play ball, and do just about anything he set his mind to. You couldn't hardly talk about him and Vern in the same breath, unless you wanted to show how far down the ladder Vern was from him.

I knew Dad wouldn't think Vern was good enough for Mom. He wouldn't want Mom to like somebody who didn't like colored people. I hoped he didn't even know about Vern. If he was dead, he couldn't do anything about it, anyway. And if he wasn't dead, Dad would come home and boot Vern out of our lives forever. And everything would be great again.

After we finished eating, Vern got up from the table and went out to the car to get his guitar.

"Can't I go, Mom?" I asked.

"No, you stay here," Mom said in a low voice. "And be nice. Tell him it's a good song."

"I thought I wasn't supposed to lie."

"This is different," she said. "Vern enjoys his music, and it's nice to say encouraging things."

Vern came back in with his guitar and we sat down in the living room.

"First I have to tune," he said, picking at a string. "Tuning's real important, Charlie. You listen, now, and someday I'll teach you how to play the guitar."

I rolled my eyes, and Mom gave me a stern look.

"Okay, here we go," Vern announced. "I wrote it for you, darlin'."

"Thank you, Vern," Mom said.

He strummed the strings a few times and sang.

"When I look at your face,
I feel so funny inside.
I get jealous sometimes,
And that's real hard to hide.
When you say you can't see me,
It cuts just like a knife.

And I'll tell you right here and now,
You're the sparkplug of my life.
Sparkplug, sparkplug—
Sparkplug of my life."

He stopped, and I looked at Mom. She put a smile on her face. "Why, thank you, Vern," she said. "That was nice. Wasn't it, Charlie?"

"It was real interesting" was all I could say.

"It was thoughtful of you to write it for me," Mom told Vern.

"That's just the first verse," he said. "I'll write three or four more before it's finished."

She nodded. "I'd like to hear the other verses when you're finished writing them."

"You like the 'sparkplug of my life' part?" he asked. "You think that's too corny?"

"Well—it's very imaginative," Mom said.

"You see, 'sparkplug of my life' is what's called a metaphor, Charlie," Vern said. "All good songs have metaphors in 'em."

"That a fact?" I said. I didn't know if that was true, but I didn't care one way or the other. That was the worst song I ever heard in my life.

"Okay if I go outside now?" I asked.

"Sure, hon," Mom said. "But be sure to stay within calling distance."

"Uh, wait just a minute, Charlie," Vern said. He put his guitar beside him on the davenport. "I want to talk to you man to man."

My body went kind of stiff. If he gave me advice, I was going to do the exact opposite of whatever he told me.

Mom looked at him funny, and he said, "You stay here, too, Mary. You should hear this."

He looked real serious, cleared his throat, and shifted on the davenport. "Charlie," he said, like he was careful about choosing his words, "the last time I was here, there was a colored man sitting at your kitchen table."

Anger boiled up inside of me and rushed out of my mouth. "His name is Luther Peale."

"Vern—" Mom began.

"No, Mary, this is something I have to say. Charlie, you ought not to be socializing with those people."

"What people are you talking about?" I asked Vern, as if I didn't know.

"Vern," Mom said, "there's nothing wrong with Charlie and Luther being friends. He's been very nice to Charlie."

"I'm sure he's nice enough," Vern said to Mom. "That's not what I'm talking about. Charlie, I'm talking about people like that who're beneath you. It isn't right. You should be looking for ways to better yourself, to come *up* in the community."

I was never so mad, but I kept myself in control. I gritted my teeth. "Don't say bad stuff about Luther. He's my friend," I said.

"Now, I'm not racially prejudiced, Charlie," Vern said, ignoring me. "But he's a *colored* man. I don't expect you to understand now, but when you're older you will. They're not the same as us."

"They are, too," I said. My voice was getting louder. "Everybody's the same. Dad told me so. And Luther's the nicest person I've met in a *long* time."

I looked at Vern hard so he'd know I was including him in the folks who didn't measure up to Luther.

Vern looked hurt and kind of mad, too, but I didn't care. He looked at Mom.

"Mary, I'm just trying to help the boy. You know that."

"Go along outside," Mom said to me softly. "I'll call you in an hour, so stay in the yard."

I stomped out the front door and let the screen slam shut behind me. Then I sat under the maple tree in front and stewed about Vern.

I didn't understand people like him. Vern didn't know anything about Luther, so how could he decide that Luther's not as good as me?

Besides, I wasn't about to let Vern tell me who I should be friends with. I really wanted to see Luther. I wanted to talk to him about baseball and Lobo and Vern and everything. I wasn't going to tell him what Vern said about him, but maybe he could tell me what to say to Mom so she'd stop seeing Vern.

I couldn't leave the yard now, but a plan was working in my mind.

Mom called me in after a while and I went to bed. She seemed tense, but Vern acted like everything was fine. I lay there in the dark and listened for him to leave.

Finally, about ten-thirty, I heard the front door open. Mom said, "'Bye, Vern. See you soon."

The door closed, and I turned over and faced the wall. Mom came in, and I could feel her standing over me, but I played possum. She tucked the covers around me, and then she left.

After another half hour, when I knew Mom was in bed and probably asleep, I got up and pulled on my jeans, a T-shirt, and sneakers.

It was a warm night, and my window was open. I pushed out the screen, climbed over the sill, and dropped soft onto the ground below.

I stood next to the house and took in a big breath of the night air to calm myself. I'd never snuck out of the house like this before, and my heart was beating wild. I knew if Mom found out I was gone, she'd go berserk, call the neighbors, call the police, call the FBI, maybe. I had to get back without her finding out.

I turned and looked around the yard. The moon was full and gave off a light that made the grass shine silver and the shadows from the overhead leaves stretch out in dark shapes across the lawn. Feeling part scared and part excited, I set off toward the river and Luther's camp.

Chapter Six

I walked straight out of Stumptown and down to the river road, the moon lighting my way. Someone had mowed his grass nearby. I like that good, clean smell because it usually means summertime when there's no school. Cut grass smells like freedom to me.

Nobody's outside much this time of night, and the street was deserted. The only sounds were the crickets in the grass and the breeze whispering through the trees overhead. Once, the headlights of a car stabbed the darkness a block away, so I ducked behind a tree in case someone in the car knew me and my mom. I didn't want them asking Mom if I was supposed to be out so late.

I came to the slope above Luther's camp and made my way down the path through the trees.

When I came to the clearing, I called out, "Luther? Are you here?"

Nobody answered.

Luther's lean-to was a dark smudge in the shadows

near the river. I walked up to it slow so I wouldn't startle him if he was asleep.

"Luther?"

"What? Charlie?" I turned and saw Luther's shadowy form sitting on the tree stump outside his lean-to.

He stood up and set something on the stump, then came toward me.

"Hi, Luther." It was good to see him.

"Does your mama know you're out this late?" he asked.

"Well..." I didn't want to lie, but if I told him no, I was positive he'd send me home right away. "I wanted to talk to you."

He stopped in front of me. "I asked you, boy, if your mama knows you're here."

He knew the truth.

"No," I said. "But I won't stay long, okay? I just wanted to see you."

"I'd like to see you, too, Charlie," Luther said, "but not when you sneak out. I don't want your mama mad at me."

I looked past him at the stump where he'd been sitting. "What are you doing?"

"Got me a crystal set," Luther said. "I was listenin' to the Cardinals game. They're playin' the Cubs tonight."

"Really?" I asked. Excitement bloomed inside me. "You're listening to the game?"

Sometimes after I went to bed at night, Dad and

Mom would listen to ball games on the radio out in the living room.

"Where'd you get the crystal set?" I asked him. Will's brother tried making one once, but it didn't work too good.

"I made it," Luther said. "Brought it with me. It's just an old Quaker Oats box, a crystal, and some wires and stuff."

"And you can pull in the Cardinals?" I asked. "All the way from St. Louis?"

"On a good night," Luther answered. "Your town has a strong radio station nearby."

"Where's the antenna?"

He turned and pointed. "There's a wire strung between two trees over there."

I laughed. "I thought that was where you dried your clothes."

"That *is* where I dry my clothes, but it's an antenna, too." I could see Luther smiling. His white teeth shone under the moonlight. "Want to listen for a minute to the game?" he asked me. "Then you gotta go."

"Yeah, I'd like that," I said.

I followed Luther to the stump.

"Sit down there," he said. I thought I smelled liquor on him, but he seemed okay. He handed me the earpiece and I listened.

"I don't hear nothing," I told him.

"It fades in and out," Luther said. "Give it a minute."

Then I heard it. A little voice off in the distance. I

couldn't hear what it was saying. But in a few seconds it got louder, and pretty soon I heard the announcer yell out, "And Musial jacks one out of the park!"

"I can hear it," I whispered. "Stan the Man just hit a home run!"

Luther beamed in the darkness. He reached down to pick up a bottle on the ground and moved a little ways off. Then he sat on the ground and leaned against a tree. "Pretty nice, ain't it? No electricity and no batteries, it don't cost a thing. Just comin' through the air and wires for free."

Luther took a drink from the bottle and wiped his mouth with the back of his hand.

"I shouldn't oughta drink in front of you, Charlie," he said. "Your mama wouldn't like it. Don't you ever take up drinkin'. It's not a good habit to get into, y'know."

"I know," I said. "I'm not plannin' on it."

The game had faded out again, and I put the crystal set on the ground at my feet. I wanted to hear the game, but I was more interested in talking to Luther. I was afraid he'd make me go home, so I said real fast, "Luther, would you tell me about meeting Jackie Robinson?"

"Okay. You ever hear of Satchel Paige?"

"Sure," I said. "He's a great pitcher."

"Well," Luther said, "I faced 'em both back in forty-five when I was playing for the Memphis Mockingbirds. What a game that was!"

He stopped and took another swallow before going

on. "Satchel was pitching. Our number three hitter nubbed one off the end of the bat, and it spun around in the grass like a crazy top for our only base hit. It was a lucky hit, too, 'cause with Satchel's arm, he could prob'ly throw a strawberry through a freight train."

"Wow," I said.

Luther laughed. "Satch didn't throw nothin' but smoke that night," he said. "When he fired his fastball, it hit the catcher's pud and cracked like a dry stick somebody stomped on. If he would've had a changeup, why, our hitters would've fallen on their faces in the dirt. And if he had other pitches, we didn't see 'em. Fact is, we hardly saw *any* of the pitches. Looked like he was throwin' aspirin tablets, they come so fast."

Luther drank again from his bottle. I didn't even want to breathe and remind Luther I was here so he'd send me home. I just wanted to hear more.

"We had some pretty fair country hitters," Luther said. "But Satch sawed 'em off on the inside, high and tight. We broke five bats that night. Manager seemed more worried about where we was goin' to get the money to buy more bats than what Satchel was doin' to our hitters. He was annihilatin' 'em!"

"And Jackie Robinson was there, too?" I asked.

"Yeah," Luther said. "He was the best stick I ever saw, Charlie. Nobody—and I mean *nobody*—could get a fastball by him. "I was young o' course, but I could throw heat with the best of 'em. But first time up, Jackie hit a frozen rope, right up the gut. It went over my head—sounded like bacon sizzlin'. The ball tore up the air and kept risin' like a kite into the sky till it disappeared into no-man's-land behind the center-field fence. I mean, he creamed it. So much for Luther Peale's best fastball in the state of Tennessee! Jackie owned it—and he owned me, too. It was *somethin'*. That ball could only have been caught by one of the dippers up there in the sky."

He laughed low in his throat.

"The second time Jackie come up," he said, "I laid my slider right on the outside corner just below the knee. That was the best slider I ever threw. Jackie banana-sliced it down the right field line—it was a chalk shot. It careened out of the corner, heading toward short center field, and passed the charging right fielder. And that was all she wrote."

Luther smiled and shook his head. "It was a standin' up inside-the-parker. Ol' Jackie didn't even break stride. Third base coach was revolvin' his arm like a windmill in a tornado, hollerin' 'Go! Go! Go!' And the on-deck hitter, with his palms turned toward the sky, was pumping them up and down like he was liftin' air, sayin', 'Stand up! Stand up!'"

A sound like a laugh came out of me. That's when I realized I was leaning as far forward on the stump as I could without falling off.

"I'm tellin' you, Charlie, Jackie had *wheels*. His legs

looked like tree trunks on the top and fence posts on the bottom. And he run just a little pigeon-toed, too. But he was *flyin'* around those sacks. He touched every base on the inside corner. That dirt was spittin' from his cleats like grass out the back of a fresh-sharpened lawn mower."

The way Luther described things, I could see it all happening in my mind.

"I do have somethin' to be grateful for that night," Luther said. "In the eighth inning, with three ducks on the pond and two outs, Jackie was due up. Well, the sky opened up like Niagara Falls. Game was called. Four-zip."

He laughed, took another drink, and leaned his head back against the tree.

"You were lucky to play against Satchel and Jackie," I said.

"Sure was."

"How'd you hurt your arm?" I asked him.

He didn't say nothing for so long, I wondered if he would answer. I couldn't see him too good while he sat in the shadows, and I even wondered if he'd gone to sleep.

But after a minute, he said, "Well, Charlie, I guess I ought to tell you the truth about that."

The way he said it made me curious. I had a feeling there was something bad tied up with what happened.

"It was an exhibition game we were playin' against the Nashville Lions. They're a white team—barnstormers, they call 'em. They travel around and play other teams.

"I was pitchin'. A player by the name of Sam Brody come up to bat. He'd been drinkin' and was pretty well gone." Luther held up his bottle. "Tennessee moonshine, Charlie. It's powerful stuff. Like I said, don't ever get started."

I shook my head and said it again. "I won't."

"Well, this Sam Brody come up to bat, an' he was so snockered, he couldn't hardly stand up straight. He was tauntin' me, callin' me names, bad names. I threw him a fastball—like I said, I was a powerful pitcher—but his head was hangin' over the plate, and the ball hit him hard right in the head. It was a good pitch—not wild. The ump called a strike, and Sam Brody dropped like a sack o' bricks on the ground."

"Was he hurt bad?" I asked.

Luther sat quiet for a minute. When he started talking again, I noticed that his words were getting slurred together.

"Sam's brother was there," Luther said. "Ruckus was his name. Or nickname, I guess. He made a ruckus wherever he went, they told me. Well, Ruckus Brody come up and started yellin' at me, threatenin' to kill me. By this time, the sheriff was there. The ump told the sheriff it was a good pitch. So the sheriff took me off a ways and said, 'I suggest you make yourself scarce for a while.'

"I went home, but that night, a player come by and

told me Sam died at the hospital, and Ruckus was comin' after me. My daddy give me some money and told me to get goin'. So I hopped a freight train comin' this way, and I jumped off here in Holden."

I tried to put all this together in my mind. "What about your arm?" I asked.

In the dim light, I saw Luther shrug his big shoulders. "I don't know, Charlie," he said quietly. "Ever since I threw that pitch that killed Sam Brody, I haven't been able to move it so good."

So he couldn't play ball anymore. That must have made him feel even more terrible.

"I'm sorry about your arm," I said. "But you didn't mean to kill Sam. He was drunk, and you threw a good pitch."

"Yeah," Luther said. He sighed heavily. "But I can't get used to the idea that I killed a man, even by accident." He held up the bottle. "I didn't start drinkin' this stuff until that day."

He got quiet again. I sat there and tried to think of what to say. Nothing came into my head. I finally decided to change the subject, so I said, "I have some of my dad's war medals from Korea. He was with the 9th Infantry Regiment. He saved a friend's life when they were fighting near the Naktong River. You want to come over sometime and see his medals?"

But Luther didn't answer. He was asleep, still leaning against the tree and snoring. I got up and went over to him.

"Get up, Luther," I said, "I'll help you to the lean-to." He stirred and muttered something. "Come on," I whispered.

I pulled at him till he got to his feet, grumbling words I couldn't understand. He leaned heavy on my shoulder, and we walked slow over to the lean-to. I felt a blanket under my feet and had him lie down.

"'Night, Luther," I said when he was on the ground. "Thanks for tellin' me about Satchel and Jackie."

He muttered again and breathed heavy in his sleep. I stood up.

"It was good seein' you again," I said, even though I knew he couldn't hear me.

Then I walked out of the lean-to, climbed the slope, and headed for home.

Chapter Seven

The heat the next day was terrible. By noon it was nearly ninety degrees, so I walked down to the river to cool off. All the while I was thinking about Luther and what he had told me the night before about accidentally killing that hitter from the Nashville Lions.

I decided not to tell Mom about it. At least not for now. I could tell she liked Luther, but it would make her nervous. I didn't want to take the chance that she'd say I couldn't see him.

It sure was strange that after Luther hit the guy with his pitch, he couldn't use that arm anymore. How could that happen? It didn't make sense to me.

I decided to go to the storm sewer to see if anyone was there. It's the place where the rainwater from the streets in this part of town dumps into the river. The mouth of the storm sewer is about twelve foot across. It's a huge, round opening made of cement and bricks. It goes back into a steep slope and turns into a tunnel under the streets of Holden.

A little ways inside, the storm sewer gets smaller and is made of cement tiles. It's still big enough that I can run through it for a while, though. I've followed it underground for about a half mile till it gets so small, I have to crawl. Every block or so, there's a manhole overhead, so I can climb out whenever I feel like it.

Mom wouldn't like it if she knew.

The best reason for spending time in the storm sewer during the summer is that it's real cool, even better than movie-theater air conditioning. Most of us Stumptown kids head down there on the hottest summer days and hang around at the mouth of it where all that cold air heaves out of the ground.

Will, Johnny, and Eileen were there when I got to the river. I felt a little bit funny seeing Will. He said, "Hey, Charlie," with the rest of them, but then he looked away.

I said hey back. I wondered if he was sorry he didn't stick up for me yesterday against Lobo. Maybe he was wondering if I'd bring it up.

They had pulled our two wooden planks out of the brush and set them over the curving damp bottom of the storm sewer floor so they could sit in comfort. We found those planks in a ditch three summers ago. They're both wide enough to seat two people. Eileen and Johnny had one, and Will sat on the other.

"Come on and sit down, Charlie," Eileen said, so I sat on Will's plank. He sort of smiled and moved over to give me more room.

Eileen had short, dark hair, and she was pretty. I'd never thought about what she looked like until one day about two weeks ago when she was playing second base. She dove for a ball that Finn threw her, and she landed with her stomach over the base a half-second before my toe touched a corner of it under her armpit. She sat up, laughing, and her eyes narrowed to little crescent moons. That's when I noticed that she'd gotten pretty sometime since the last time I looked at her. I was surprised, seeing that. She'd always been one of the guys, though, and that's the way she wanted it.

"Hey, Charlie," Johnny said. "You seen Lobo since yesterday? All of us were just talkin' about what happened."

My stomach lurched at the sound of Lobo's name. Will was watching me, but he turned his head again when I looked over at him. I thought he seemed ashamed. That made me feel a little better.

Johnny laughed. "Boy, you sure clobbered him, Charlie!" he said. "He got what was comin' to him, that's for sure."

"No, I haven't seen him," I said. Then I turned to Will and said, "You like playin' ball with him?"

He shrugged. "Lobo's a good player." He rubbed a spot of dirt on the plank we were sitting on. "But he can be a jerk sometimes."

"You mean, sometimes he's *not* a jerk?" Eileen asked.

Will gave out a sudden laugh like he hadn't meant

to. He glanced up at me for a second. "He shouldn'ta picked on you guys yesterday."

Eileen did the talking for me. "How come you didn't tell him to cut it out?" she asked.

Will hesitated, and Johnny chimed in. "Heck, Lobo woulda *killed* Will if he had."

"That right?" I asked him. "Would he've killed you?"

Will shrugged. "Maybe." He frowned then, and said almost in a whisper, "Sorry I didn't say anything."

Those were about the best words he could say. Will must have been a little scared of Lobo, too, and I couldn't blame him. Besides, they were playing on the same team now.

"It's okay," I said. "I sure hope he don't make good on his threat, though, and kill me." It came out sounding too much like a little kid, so I said like I was joking, "But I got my PF Flyers on just in case."

Eileen laughed. "Yeah, you might need to 'run faster and jump higher,' like they say on the radio." Then she added with a wave of her hand, "He's not gonna kill you, Charlie. That's just talk. He's got a mouth as big as Linn County."

"As big as the whole state of Iowa," Johnny said.

Eileen laughed. "The world."

"The universe!" I added.

I laughed along with them, but I was still scared at the thought of seeing Lobo again.

"Hey, Charlie, you were doin' some good pitching in the workup yesterday," Eileen said.

"Thanks," I replied. "I learned some stuff from a

new friend of mine. His name's Luther. You guys should meet him."

"Did he just move here?" Eileen asked.

"He's a grown-up," I said. "He was a pitcher for the Memphis Mockingbirds. They're a team in the Negro League."

"Really?" Johnny said. "Where'd you meet him?"

"At Wildcats tryouts," I said. "He was watching us."

Will nodded. "Oh, yeah, I remember seeing him sitting on the bleacher."

"So when did you start practicing with the Wildcats?" I asked him.

"Last night," he said. "Coach Hennessey's real tough, and he has favorites, like Brad Lobo. He's good at coaching, though."

"Well, look who's here!"

I jerked around to see Brad Lobo himself, with two of his buddies. They were coming down the hillside toward the river. I never see Lobo around the river because he don't live in Stumptown or even close.

I was so surprised and scared at seeing him that my mouth went dry and didn't work at first. Finally, I said—and it came out more like a whisper—"What're you doin' here?"

"What do you think?" Lobo said, sneering. "Looking for *you,* Snothead. We got a score to settle."

He stood there with his fists on his hips like he was Superman or something. I stood up, my mind racing around in circles, trying to think of a way out of this.

I stood up and glanced at Will, hoping he'd say something this time.

But it was Johnny who stuck up for me. "Come on, Lobo," he said. "It's not a fair match. You got about fifteen pounds on Charlie here."

Then Will said, "Yeah," but it came out weak and soft.

"That didn't stop him yesterday," Lobo said.

Eileen laughed. "Sure didn't."

I wished she hadn't said that, because Lobo's face turned a deep red. He started screaming and ran at me.

Without even thinking, I ran into the storm sewer, away from Lobo.

I ran as if my life depended on it, which it probably did. It's real dark underground, and after sitting in the bright sunlight, I couldn't see anything. My ears were filled with the sound of my own puffing breath and the slap of the cement under my sneakers. It smelled musty and damp, too, and every breath I pulled in felt heavy and cold.

Every now and then the sound changed a tiny bit, and I knew I was running past openings that fed into the main tunnel. I wished they were bigger so I could run into one of them, and maybe Lobo would run right past me and on up the tunnel.

I didn't turn back to see where Lobo was till I'd run about a half block underground.

Finally, still running, I whipped my head around to

look behind me. I could see the small light from the opening of the storm sewer way down at the end. I thought I'd see a silhouette of Lobo running between me and the light. But he wasn't there.

Where was he?

I stopped, breathing hard, and stared at the light. I could see Eileen, Will, and Johnny standing in the opening like small plastic soldiers. They were looking this way, I'm sure trying to see me. But it's impossible to see anything this far into the tunnel.

Lobo must not have wanted to follow me into the dark of the storm sewer. If he'd never been in it before, he probably lost his nerve.

I suddenly felt ashamed for running away. Eileen and Johnny wouldn't congratulate me this time. All I did was act like a scared rabbit, scampering down its rabbit hole. Will would probably understand, though. He'd been too scared to say much to Lobo himself.

A tiny pinpoint of light was shining from above me a little ways off. That meant there would be a manhole overhead where I could climb out.

I walked to the manhole. Above me, iron bars like giant staples were cemented into the concrete. Last summer was the first year I was tall enough to reach the lowest one. Before that, I climbed on Will's back. Anyway, I grabbed it and pulled myself up, then pushed my shoulder into the heavy manhole covering. It moved, and I shoved it to the side, climbed out, and pushed it back. I was in the field next to Hayes School.

The sunlight was blinding. It took a full minute before I could stop squinting.

I took a deep breath, and the air around me was hot and heavy. Feeling heavy myself from shame and embarrassment, I trudged home.

* * *

When I got to my front stoop, I opened the milk box and pulled out the two glass bottles. We get two quarts of milk delivered every day, and it's my job to bring them inside. It was good I remembered to bring them in right away. Even with all the insulation in the metal box, the milk would turn bad pretty fast on a day as hot as this one.

I was putting the milk in the Frigidaire when the telephone rang.

"Hello?"

"Hey, Charlie." It was Will.

"Hey." I'd been hoping he'd call, but I wasn't sure if he would. I wanted to hear what he'd say about Lobo. Maybe he'd say he didn't blame me for running, that he was kind of scared of him, too.

"You wanna get some kids together and play workup at the park later?" he asked.

It was too hot to play, but I didn't want to look like the biggest sissy in Holden, so I said, "Sure."

"Okay." Then there was a long silence.

"Hey, Will?"

"Yeah?"

"What did Lobo do? I mean, after I ran into the tunnel?" I had to know.

"Oh, he just said some stuff and left. I bet he'd never been in the storm sewer before."

"Oh."

A week ago, Will would've called him a chicken.

There was a *click* on the line. Then old Mrs. Whitley said, "Who's there?"

I sighed. "It's me, Mrs. Whitley. I'm gettin' off the phone in a second, okay?"

"Well, hurry up, then," she said. "I have to order my groceries." She hung up.

"I swear," I said to Will. "We have the crabbiest people on this party line. And they're all a bunch of busybodies. You never know who's listenin' in."

"I heard that, Charlie Nebraska!" It was Lucy Stetton, a girl in our class. Her family was on the party line with us and Mrs. Whitley.

"Get off the phone, Lucy!" I yelled at her.

"Too bad you ran away from Brad Lobo," she said before slamming the phone down hard.

Great. Now the whole town would know what a chicken I am.

"What time we playin' workup?" I asked Will.

"Four-thirty," Will said. "The McNally guys have to help their mom move furniture this afternoon so they can paint the living room."

"Okay," I said. "See you." I started to hang up. "And, um, Will?"

"Yeah?"

"I'm glad you still want to play ball with us," I said.

"Oh," Will said. "Okay. See ya." He hung up.

I'd wanted him to say, *Sure, I'd rather play with you guys.*

I wondered if he liked playing with the Wildcats better than us.

It was only two o'clock, so I had a couple hours to kill. When I heard the buzz and bells of Herman's ice cream cart, I grabbed a nickel from my bank and ran outside.

Herman has a lame leg, but he can drive his cart since it's mounted on a motorbike.

"Hey, Herman!" I called. I stopped at the curb and waved my arms.

He waggled a hand and pulled up next to me.

I don't know Herman's last name, but we always talk baseball when we do business. I never see him without his St. Louis Cardinals cap. It's dark with dirt, but he said he got it at a game in St. Louis in forty-seven and he's never throwing it away. Or washing it, either, probably. He always has stubble growing on his chin and cheeks, like he can't be bothered to shave more than every few days.

"I want a grape Popsicle, please," I said.

"That'll be a nickel," Herman said, opening the frosty top of his cart. I stuck my face in to feel the cold air, but he pushed me out of the way. "Don't breathe in there, kid. You hear the Cardinals game last night?"

"I heard when Stan Musial hit a home run," I said. "That was pretty exciting. What was the final score?"

"The Cards walloped the Cubs, six to zero," he said. He grinned and showed the hole where his front tooth should have been. He raised an eyebrow. "I hear you had to run from that Lobo kid this morning."

Geesh. Bad news travels at lightning speed around Stumptown.

"You were talkin' to Lucy just now, huh?" I said, scowling.

Herman shrugged. "She bought a Frosty Ice Cream Bar. How's your mom?"

"Fine," I said.

"She still seein' that salesman?" he asked.

I scowled again. Seemed Herman sure had to know everything. "Yeah. So?"

"They gonna get married? Your mom and the salesman? What's his name?"

"Vern Jardine," I said. "Why're you so interested?"

"Just wonderin', that's all," Herman said. "Maybe he'll adopt you, and you'll inherit all his money. You'd have to change your name, probably."

"I'd never change my name," I told him. "My dad's name is Nebraska, and that's the only name I'll ever have."

"Not if that fella adopts you." Herman got on his bike and started up his motor again. "Charlie Jardine. That's not too bad. Well, see ya."

He rode away.

I watched him go. If it wasn't for those grape Popsicles, I wouldn't care if I never saw Herman again. He's the nosiest person I ever met, and he spreads gossip like wind spreads a wildfire.

I tore the paper wrapping off the Popsicle and sat under the tree to eat it. There's nothing better on a hot day than a grape Popsicle. It fills your mouth with a sweet coldness that spreads through you and seeps into your bones for a few minutes, like the cold in the storm sewer.

This time I didn't enjoy it too much, though. I was playing over in my mind what Herman said about Vern adopting me if Mom married him. There was no way I'd ever let them change my name.

"Vern'll *never* be my dad," I said out loud to myself. *"Never."*

After the Popsicle was gone, I went inside and into my room. I picked up the snow globe my dad won for me and shook it. I lay on my bed and watched the white snow swirl around the little house.

Dad, please be alive. Come home so Mom won't marry Vern. Come home so Mom and I can be happy and everything can be like it was before you left.

My comic books are piled on a shelf above my bed. I sat up and looked through them. I lay back again and reread one of the *Superman* comics. *Captain Marvel* and *Superman* are my favorites, but *Batman, Robin*, and *Crime Does Not Pay* are good ones, too.

When I'd finished reading the comic book, I stared

up at the ceiling. I wished I was a superhero. I wished I was so fast and strong that I wouldn't be afraid of Lobo or anybody else.

If I was a superhero, I could have big adventures, saving people's lives and keeping the town safe from criminals. There would be more excitement in one day than I've had in my whole life.

That would be so great.

* * *

I fell asleep for a while and woke up at a quarter past four. I grabbed my bat and glove and hurried in the heat to Scott Park.

Everybody who'd played the day before was there, plus Will. They'd all started out in their favorite positions again, but Will was pitching because I wasn't there.

"I'm gonna pitch today, Charlie," he said. "Gotta work on my pitchin' arm."

"Okay." For the first time I wished Will hadn't made the team. Before this, if he wanted to play a certain position, he'd ask if anyone minded. This time, he *told* us.

I wondered if Coach Hennessey was going to let him pitch for the Wildcats, but I didn't ask.

I got in line to bat behind Kathleen, Leslie, and Jim.

Will wound up and pitched a good one to Kathleen.

She smacked it up to Bowie in left field. He caught it, but the ball bounced out of his glove and onto the ground. He fumbled for it while Kathleen raced for first. She was safe before Bowie was able to scoop up the ball and throw it.

Casey hollered from right field, "It's that new glove, Bowie. It don't catch the ball as good as our old ones."

Bowie nodded, but I think he was embarrassed. I mean, that fly ball Kathleen hit was a can of corn. Bowie was standing under the ball when it came right to him. He didn't hardly have to take a step to catch it.

Everybody rotated to the next position. Next up was Leslie, who's a real good hitter. Will heaved her a fastball.

She hit a grounder to Alan at shortstop. Alan fired it to Eileen on second, getting Kathleen out. Then Eileen threw it to Johnny on first, so Leslie was out.

"Great double play!" Bowie yelled. "The Wildcats couldn't have done better!"

Will hollered, "I've seen 'em do better plays than that." I guess he was feeling like a genuine Wildcat, loyal to his team.

My chest felt like something was pressing on it right then and made me feel kind of sad.

It was awful hot, but when I play baseball, I guess I forget about the temperature till I'm about ready to pass out. Sweat was rolling off my face and sliding down my back.

We'd rotated positions about ten times before I noticed Luther walking along the grass next to the baseball diamond.

"Hey, Luther!" I called. We were between plays, so I ran over to him. "How do you like the job at Landen's?"

"It's a good job, Charlie." He looked out over the ballpark. "You havin' a good time?"

"Sure," I said. "Wanna stay and watch awhile? We're playin' workup."

"Okay," Luther said.

I turned toward all the players in the field.

"Hey," I yelled. "This here's Luther Peale. He's a professional baseball player."

Luther grinned. "I *was*," he called out. "I *was* a professional."

"With the Memphis Mockingbirds," I added.

"Hey, Luther," Bowie shouted.

"Nice to meet ya!" Eileen yelled. "Charlie told us about you." Everybody else waved or hollered hello, too.

Luther grinned and waved back.

We started playing again, and Bowie dropped the first fly ball.

"It's that stupid glove again, Bowie," Alan yelled.

I was up at bat next. I was feeling pretty self-conscious because Luther was here. Will pitched a good fastball. I swung hard and missed.

"Strike one!" yelled Walter.

"Don't take your eye off that ball, Charlie," Luther

said from behind the backstop. "Talk to yourself. Say, 'I can hit it; I can hit it.'"

I nodded and got ready. "I can hit it; I can hit it."

"Watch the ball," Luther said, his voice low. "You can hit it."

The pitch came, and I slammed that ball clear out into the stratosphere.

"Wow!" Johnny yelled from first base. "You really stung that ball!"

I was too busy running for first base to see Luther's face, but I bet he was grinning. I ran the bases for the first home run of the afternoon.

Everybody pounded me on the back, and Luther came over. "See, Charlie?" he said. "You just got to watch that ball and tell yourself you can do it."

The others came in to hear what Luther was telling me.

"You havin' trouble with your glove?" Luther asked Bowie.

"Oh, it's not the glove," Bowie said. His face turned red.

"Don't be too sure," Luther said. "Let me see it."

He took the glove, slipped it on, and pounded his fist into it.

"This is a new glove," Luther said. "It needs shapin'."

"Shapin'?" Bowie asked. "How do you do that?"

"Here's what you do," Luther said. "Tonight, you go home and—you have a kitten ball?"

"A softball?" Bowie asked. "Yeah, my sisters play softball."

"Okay," Luther said. "Put the softball into the glove and tie it closed with a strip of cloth. Then let the whole thing soak in a bucket of water for a half hour or so."

"Won't that ruin the glove?" Alan asked.

"No," Luther said. "Take it out and let it dry for a day or two, still tied closed. Then—your mama got some hog lard?"

"Sure," Bowie said. "She uses it for pies 'n stuff."

"Okay," Luther said. "Then when it's dry, untie the cloth and use it to rub the glove with a little hog lard. You'll have a great glove from then on."

I looked at all the faces around me. Everyone was listening real hard. I'm sure they were thinking they'd better listen to the advice of a pro.

"Hey, Luther," Bowie said, "maybe you could be our coach."

Everybody started talking at once. Why didn't I think of that? Luther would be the perfect coach! And we wouldn't have to try out to be on the team. All us Stumptown kids could play, even the girls who weren't allowed to try out for the Wildcats.

"Will you do it?" I asked Luther. "You could make us a great team."

"Who would we play?" Jim asked.

"Luther hasn't even said he'd coach us yet!" I yelled at him. "First things first. Would you, Luther?"

A smile spread over his face. "Okay, Charlie," he said. "It'd be fun gettin' back into baseball."

So now we had ourselves a coach.

"We'll play any team that wants to play us," Luther said. "Maybe even the Wildcats."

I looked over at Will. He was the only person who wasn't smiling.

Chapter Eight

Vern, this bouquet is so pretty," Mom said at supper that night. "It must have been expensive. You really shouldn't have spent the money on it. But I love it," she added. She reached over and turned the vase to the right a little.

"Nothing but the best for my Mary," Vern said, smiling.

It made me mad the way he said it. Mom wasn't *his* Mary.

I'd been thinking a lot about what Herman said about Vern adopting me. I sat there staring at Vern, imagining what it would be like if he was here all the time.

If he tried to be my dad.

The thought of it made my stomach feel bad, like rocks were piled up in there. I was never going to be Vern's son.

"I've been thinking about something, Mary," he said. "In fact, I've given this some serious thought, and seeing as how I'm the only male influence

Charlie's got, I think I should spend some time with him a couple times a week. We could start going fishing—maybe take in a ball game now and then." He looked at me. "We'll have fun, Charlie. I'm really looking forward to it."

I wanted to say, *I don't need you for anything. I have my dad and Luther.* I nearly said it, too.

"Oh, Vern, I think that would be wonderful," Mom said. "Charlie would love to do some of the things he used to do with his dad."

What? She couldn't believe that. Maybe she was trying to make Vern feel good. But Mom was smiling, so I didn't know for sure what she was thinking.

"You smart in school, Charlie?" Vern asked. He squinted at me from across the table as if he was trying to see into my brain.

"I do okay." I'm not at the top of my class, but I'm not at the bottom, either. Anyhow, I figured it was none of his business.

"Well, it's important to work hard, but don't let anyone tell you that you've got to get straight A's," Vern said. "I didn't get too many A's, but I'm still a success. And I won't be selling vacuum cleaners all my life, either. I'm working myself up to management, and before long, I'll own the company. Then I'll sell it and buy another one—build that up and sell that one, too. That's how a man can get rich."

"That's wonderful, Vern," my mom said, patting his arm. "But an education is important. Charlie's going to graduate from high school and then maybe go on to college."

"Maybe I'll be an electrician like my dad," I added.

"Anybody can be an electrician," Vern said. "Be somebody special. Like a—"

"My dad was special!" Now I was really mad.

"Bill was a very special man," Mom said, frowning at Vern. "Charlie looked up to Bill a lot. We both did, and so did everybody who knew him. He was an excellent father and a wonderful man." She looked back and forth between me and Vern. "But I think it's a great idea for you two to spend more time together. In fact, why don't you both go outside now, and Vern, you can pitch a few balls to Charlie while I clean up. It'll only take ten minutes or so."

"Sure," Vern said. "I'll give you some pointers, Charlie."

"You gonna play ball in your suit?" I asked.

He'd taken off his jacket when he came in, but he still wore a shirt, tie, and pants. I didn't care if he wrecked his clothes. I just didn't want to play ball with him. I figured Vern probably didn't know a fastball from the nose on his face, and I didn't feel like teaching him.

"We'll just hit a few until your mom's finished cleaning up."

I almost said I didn't feel like it, but Mom had a hopeful look, so I changed my mind. I guessed I could stand a few minutes of it.

"Okay." I made sure I didn't sound too happy about it, though.

"I'll be out in the backyard," Vern said. He probably played so bad he didn't want anyone to see him from the street.

I got my bat, ball, and glove from my closet and walked through the kitchen on my way to the back door.

Mom stood in front of the sink, running hot water for dishes. "Have fun," she said, smiling.

I couldn't imagine having fun with Vern, but I didn't say it. I went outside.

Vern started calling out instructions right off. "Here's the pitching mound," he said, tapping a spot between me and the bush next to the kitchen window.

"Mom'll want me to hit away from the house," I told him.

He rolled his eyes and smiled as if it was him and me against Mom. "O-kay. We sure don't want Mary to worry about broken windows." He took the ball and glove from me and walked farther out into the yard. "We'll play sideways. You can hit into the neighbor's yard."

That was Mrs. Banks's yard. I wondered if she was watching now like the night Luther came for supper. I couldn't see her standing in the window. Watching us play ball probably wasn't as interesting as watching me and Mom fight about a colored man.

"Ready?" Vern asked.

I nodded and got ready to swing.

Vern threw a wild ball that went left and dropped into Mrs. Banks's yard. I ran over and picked up the ball and tossed it back to him.

"Watch now," he said.

He wound up again and pitched me a ball that flew over my head about four feet.

I thought Vern would be embarrassed by that awful pitch, but he just shrugged, and I went to get the ball. I threw it back to him, but he muffed it and it landed at his feet. I sighed. This was going to be a long ten minutes. I wondered how many of the minutes had passed yet. Maybe Mom was watching from the window over the sink, and she'd have mercy on me and hurry with the dishes.

"You want to trade places?" I asked him. "I'll pitch you some balls."

"Sure," he said. "Whatever will be helpful to you."

Helpful to *me? Geesh.* This was trying my patience something awful. We traded places, and I pitched him one right over the plate. He swung hard and missed.

"Throw a good pitch now," he said, going to get it. "That was too low." He threw it back.

I gritted my teeth. "It was perfect," I murmured real soft. So ol' Vern wanted to be my male influence? He was more like a model of a person you'd *never* want to be like.

I gave him an underhand pitch. He swung and connected with the ball. It flew at an angle and crashed through Mrs. Banks's shed window.

Vern stood there with his mouth open, looking at the broken shards of glass still clinging to the window frame. He looked back at me and put a finger to his lips, then strolled with his hands in his pockets toward the shed. Mrs. Banks didn't come out, so I figured she wasn't home or didn't see what happened.

Mom didn't come out either. Maybe she didn't hear it.

Vern stopped in front of the shed, opened the door, and disappeared inside. In ten seconds he was out again, the ball in his hand, closing the door behind him. He walked over to me.

"I have a better idea, Charlie," he said. "Let's me, you, and your mom go get some ice cream."

"But aren't you going to—"

"Why don't we keep this our little secret," Vern said. He put a hand on my shoulder as we walked toward the back door.

"What do you mean?" I gave him a hard stare. "You aren't going to pay Mrs. Banks for a new window?"

"Let's just forget about it." He squeezed my shoulder, and I jerked away from him. "It wasn't a good pitch, Charlie." Vern said. "Nobody could've hit that ball."

Ever since supper when I thought about Vern adopting me, I'd been holding in all my bad feelings about him. His rotten pitches had made me even madder, but now the broken window and trying to weasel out of paying for it made me feel all crazy inside.

Vern said, "I'll have to coach you a little bit so you know a good pitch from a bad one, son."

I opened my mouth and something in my head yelled, *Don't tell him!* But the storm inside me had to have someplace to go. All I wanted to do was make Vern miserable.

I stopped at the back door and looked Vern Jardine straight in the eyes. "I already know a good pitch from a bad one, Vern. Luther's coachin' us in baseball. Up until a little while ago, he was a *professional* baseball player in Tennessee. See, he's an expert, and he's giving us lots of good advice. So I don't need *you* tellin' me *nothin'*."

Vern tilted his head a little like he didn't hear me right. "You're playin' baseball with that colored fella?"

I nodded. It felt good to see the bright red rising up in his face. "We're real good friends," I added.

Vern pushed me inside and through the kitchen. "Mary!" he called.

Mom hurried out of her bedroom with a hairbrush in her hand. "I'm right here," she answered. "What's wrong?"

I didn't care what Vern said to Mom. He could yell himself into the next county, but he wasn't my dad and he never would be. Luther was my "male influence" since Dad's not here, and I was going to see him whenever I wanted to.

Vern pointed at me. "Did you know Charlie's still seein' that colored fella?"

"Well, yes," Mom said. I could tell she was upset, but she kept looking at me as if that helped her talk.

"Luther's a nice young man. He's teaching the kids a lot about baseball."

"Why didn't you tell me?"

"'Cause it was none of your business, Vern," I said.

Mom gasped and turned to me, her eyes filled with surprise. "Charlie, don't you talk that way!"

But I was too mad to stop. "You're not my dad, Vern." My voice was getting louder and louder. "You got no say about who I can have for a friend."

"Go to your room, Charlie," Mom said. Her eyes were angry and her voice was louder than I'd ever heard it.

"Ask Vern about Mrs. Banks's shed window," I told her. "Ask him why he won't pay for it after he broke it."

I stomped into my room and slammed the door behind me.

Then I flopped on my bed and put my hands under my head and glared up at the ceiling.

I could hear Mom and Vern talking in low voices in the living room.

"What's this about Mrs. Banks—"

"Mary, I mean what I say here," Vern interrupted. "Are the other parents allowing this?"

"Vern," Mom said, "I can't tell Charlie not to see Luther. They're friends, and I—"

"I thought I was going to help you raise that boy," Vern said.

"What?"

Yeah, what? I sat up and listened hard.

Vern said, "Don't be so surprised, Mary. You know how I feel about you. You're the most wonderful woman I've ever known: beautiful and smart and sweet. I want to guide the boy. He needs a man to teach to him things—and not a colored man, either."

"Vern, I know you're doing what you think is right, but you haven't given Luther a chance. You're judging him before—"

"I know you think I'm prejudiced," Vern said. "But I'm not."

"But Vern, you're judging Luther without knowing him," Mom said in a patient voice. "He's a nice young man, and he's been good to Charlie—"

"You're not listening to me," Vern said real loud.

"Let's not talk about this now," Mom said. She sounded tired and lowered her voice. "I don't want to fight with you, Vern."

I slid off the bed and walked real quiet to the door to listen more closely.

Vern said in a softer voice, "I don't want to fight, either, Mary. But we've got to get this settled. I'm not having a boy of mine makin' friends and spending time with a colored man."

My ears pricked up at that. *A boy of mine?*

Mom heard it, too. "What did you say?" she asked.

"I said—well, he's like my boy, Mary," Vern said. "You know how much I care about both of you. And maybe you and me will get married one of these days."

"Are you proposing, Vern?" Mom asked.

"You know I love you, Mary," he said.

They said some stuff real low that I couldn't hear. I put my ear to the door. There wasn't a sound for a long time, so I twisted the doorknob and peeked out.

Vern was kissing my mom.

I felt sick to my stomach.

I closed the door and lay back down on my bed. If Mom married Vern, I didn't know what I'd do.

And what would happen if Dad *was* alive over in North Korea? What if he came home to find out that Mom had gone and married somebody else? And Mom and I had different last names than he did?

It hurt too much to even think about it.

I hated Vern Jardine with a red-hot hatred. And I was ready to do anything I could to make sure Mom never married him.

* * *

A while later, Mom tapped on my door. She opened it and came in and sat on my bed. I held my breath, waiting to hear what she'd say.

"Charlie, I know how you feel about Luther," she said. "I like Luther, too. He's a good man."

"You're not gonna tell me I can't see him, are you?"

"No," Mom said. "That wouldn't be right."

"Good." I could feel some of my stomach muscles unclenching.

"But Charlie, you shouldn't have yelled at Vern. I've taught you better than that."

I didn't say anything.

"I want you to apologize to Vern," Mom said.

"But he's not my dad," I argued. "He can't tell me who I can be friends with."

"That's true, but you still don't have the right to be disrespectful," she said. "Vern means well." She reached out and smoothed my hair. "Come on, honey. Vern's going to take us to get ice cream."

"I don't want any," I said.

"Since when?" Mom asked. "Ice cream's your favorite food."

"Mom, please don't marry Vern! He'd make me stop seein' Luther. And what if Dad really isn't dead?"

The words just came out of my mouth. Mom looked real surprised.

"Honey, I'm sorry. Your dad *is*...gone."

I tried to keep the tears from coming, but they came anyway. "But what if they made a mistake?"

"Oh, sweetheart," Mom said. Now her eyes filled up with tears, and she took my hand. "Dad's body was identified by the Army. I wish it was a mistake, too, with all my heart. But it wasn't, Charlie. It wasn't a mistake."

"You didn't look yourself and see if it was Dad," I said. "So you don't know for sure."

"It was your dad," Mom said, her voice real quiet. "There was no doubt, honey."

I didn't believe it. I knew it was still possible there was a mistake. But I could see pretty clear that I couldn't convince her.

Mom quickly brushed at her eyes. "You can still see Luther," she said. "I promise you that. Now, come on."

"Vern's nothing like Dad," I said in a quieter voice.

"No, he's not," she said. "But you *will* be civil to him."

"He broke Mrs. Banks's window—"

"He explained to me about Mrs. Banks and her window, and he's going to pay for it. Now, come on."

Mom nudged me and I got up and followed her into the living room. Vern was standing there puffing on a cigarette.

"Charlie has something he wants to say," Mom told him. "Go on, Charlie."

"Sorry I yelled," I mumbled. It was the same kind of lie I told him when I said he wrote a good song. A lie to keep Mom happy.

"Well, Charlie," Vern said. "I just want to steer you in the right direction. Because I care about you, son. You know that, don't you?"

I didn't answer. Instead I walked past him and out the screen door.

I crossed the yard to the maple tree and sat down under it.

Thinking about Vern made me feel sick. I hated him for kissing my mom. I almost even hated my mom for liking him. And I hated the way he talked about Luther and all the other colored people in the world.

I leaned my head back against the tree. If only Dad would come home. I bet he and Luther would be friends.

I thought I'd gotten over the worst part of missing my dad. But today I missed him so much, my chest ached more than ever.

* * *

The next afternoon, just before five o'clock, I headed toward Landen's to wait for Luther. He'd called me to say he found a place where he could stay. It was a room in a boardinghouse not too far from Stumptown. I said I'd help him move his stuff from the lean-to to his room.

Luther really didn't need help, seeing as how he could stuff all the things he owned into that gunny-sack of his. But it was a chance to spend some more time with him.

I was a little disappointed he was leaving his camp because it was such a great place. But when he told me it rained last night and he got soaked and cold, I was happy he'd be more comfortable with a real roof over his head.

When I got to Landen's, the big door was standing open. I pulled open the screen door and went inside. Four ladies were lined up at the counter, waiting to sell their eggs. They were all carrying small wooden crates with handles on top.

Luther was on the other side of the counter with Mr. Landen. He was so busy he didn't see me at first. I walked around the ladies and went to the far edge of the counter.

After a minute or so, Luther looked up and smiled. "I'll be with you in a bit, Charlie," he said.

I nodded and leaned against the counter to wait.

The lady who was first in line at the counter handed Luther her box.

Mr. Landen looked up from his paperwork near the cash register. "You want to watch Luther candle eggs, Charlie?" he asked.

"Sure," I said.

"Come around the counter."

Luther took the lady's box, glanced over at me, and nodded toward a back room. I followed Luther into the room and we stopped at a large table at the side. Sitting on the table was a contraption that had a metal frame and two holes in the top. A strong light shone out of the holes.

Luther opened the lady's egg box and carefully took out the top tray of eggs. He whisked the eggs by twos out of the cardboard tray, held them up to the two lit holes, then put them into different trays that sat to the side on the table.

"Why're you doing that?" I asked him.

"Making sure they're not rotten or don't have chicks in 'em," Luther said.

"How can you tell?" I asked.

"See," he said, pausing with two eggs. "You don't want to see shadows when you hold 'em up to the light. If they're bad or have chicks, you'll see shadows."

I didn't see any shadows.

He finished candling the eggs in no time—he only

found one egg with a shadow in the whole six dozen—and went to the woman at the counter and gave her back her empty box. Mr. Landen wrote up a slip of paper for the eggs, then paid the lady from the cash register.

When Luther took the next lady's eggs, I said, "I'll wait outside for you." He nodded, and I went to wait on the sidewalk.

I sat on Landen's front stoop. It wasn't so hot today, and the street was busy with cars. People were going home from where they worked downtown.

Four guys scuffed along the sidewalk about a half block away, yelling at cars going by, but I didn't pay much attention to them. I was watching an ant carry a piece of bread three times its size along the sidewalk. I wished I was so strong I could lift something three times my size. Ants are like little Supermans. They do things that seem impossible when you really think about them.

I was paying so much attention to the ant, I didn't know what was happening till four pairs of sneakers stopped in front of me.

"Hey, Stumptown. Whatcha doin'?" Lobo asked. "Watchin' a stupid ant? Guess that makes you pretty stupid, too."

He brought his foot down hard and squashed the ant and its load of bread. Then he laughed.

I squinted up at Lobo, my heart doing the crazy dance it does every time I see him. I was mad because he killed that innocent ant, but I was also pretty scared, if you want to know the truth.

"You shoulda seen Stumptown run away from me yesterday, he was so scared," Lobo told his friends. "Ran right into the storm sewer!" His friends laughed.

I stood up and I could feel my legs shaking.

"We got a score to settle, Stumptown," Lobo said, pushing his face into mine.

I guess I was still feeling pretty bad about running away the last time, because I stood my ground even though I was scared. "I'm tired of you callin' me Stumptown," I said. "My name is Charlie."

Lobo laughed. "Well, too bad, 'cause Stumptown's all I'm callin' you."

He gave me a hard shove, and I slammed back into Landen's door. Lobo grabbed me by my shirt and pushed me off the step, onto the cement sidewalk. He fell down on top of me and started punching me in the ribs.

Suddenly an arm reached down and hauled Lobo off me. I scrambled to my feet.

"That's enough," Luther said in a big voice. He had a good hold of Lobo's shirt. After a few seconds, he let go.

Lobo whirled around to Luther. "Who're you?" he said. "This ain't none of your business."

"It is when you're chasin' off customers," Luther said. "And besides, Charlie here is a friend of mine."

A sneer worked its way over Lobo's face. "I shoulda known. Stumptown has a colored friend."

I wanted to punch him hard for trying to hurt Luther's feelings. I lunged at Lobo, but Luther grabbed me. He didn't look hurt or mad. He said in a serious voice, "You boys can settle this on the baseball diamond."

"Huh?" I said.

I frowned at Luther and gave him signals with my eyes to tell him this was a very bad idea. But he didn't seem to get it.

Lobo snorted. "You want the Wildcats to play Stumptown and his girlfriends? We'll kill 'em!"

Yeah, Luther, I thought. *They'll kill us.*

"That's right," Luther said calmly. "Charlie's team plays you and your team. In three weeks at Scott Park."

Three weeks? Was Luther crazy?

Lobo said, "Sure. You got yourself a deal, Stumptown. Three weeks." He snorted. "We'll beat you so bad, everybody in Holden'll be splitting their pants laughing."

I looked at Luther again. He had a little smile on his face.

Great, I thought. *In three weeks, all us Stumptown kids will be so embarrassed, we'll want to leave town. But maybe that's better than getting killed.*

Then again, maybe it isn't.

Chapter Nine

Luther, we can't beat Brad Lobo and those guys at baseball," I said as we walked along the sidewalk toward the river. My insides were all jumpy. "They're the best players in Holden. They'll beat us bad."

"Now what kind of thinkin' is that?" Luther said.

"Honest thinking," I said.

"Well, that's where we'll start, then," Luther said. "A whole lot of baseball is played in the mind, Charlie. Remember at practice yesterday when you didn't hit the ball? Your swing was wild. But as soon as you concentrated on watching that ball and you said out loud you could hit it, you creamed it."

"Yeah, well, it'll be different when we're playin' against Lobo and a bunch of great ballplayers."

"Now that's what I'm talkin' about, Charlie," Luther said. "You should play just as good in front of Lobo as you do in front of me."

I looked up at Luther walking along beside me. "That would take a miracle. Geesh. I'm already scared, and I got three more weeks to think about it."

Luther smiled. "You'll do just fine, Charlie."

When we got to his camp at the river, we gathered up his things and put them in the gunnysack.

"It's a good thing nobody came along and took everything," I told him.

"Nobody'd want this stuff," Luther said.

"What about your crystal set?" I asked.

He shrugged. "Most people would look at the oat box and the wires wrapped around it and say, 'What's this piece of junk?'"

"Yeah, if they didn't know what it could do," I said. "Like pull in a ball game from clear down in St. Louis!"

We climbed up the slope and started off toward the boardinghouse. Luther carried the gunnysack over his shoulder. I lugged two of his old blankets to lighten his load a bit.

"That Lobo fella sure seems to have it in for you," Luther said.

"That's 'cause I flattened him the other day," I told him. "I didn't even think about what I was doing. He started after Walter, who's not very tough, and it just made me mad."

Luther nodded. We stopped at the corner and crossed the street. "It was nice of you to stick up for your friend."

"Well, if I get points for doing good then," I said, "I'd have to lose a couple for running away the next day. Lobo came after me, and I ran like a scared rabbit into the storm sewer to get away from him."

"Nothin' wrong with that, Charlie," Luther said. "Fighting never solved nothin', anyway."

"I was a coward," I said, my voice low.

"No, you were wise, Charlie," Luther said. "You fought to protect someone weaker who couldn't defend himself. But you avoided a fight when Lobo came after you."

I knew Luther was trying to make me feel better. But I still felt bad about being such a chicken.

We got to the boardinghouse a few minutes later. It was a huge white house with a big porch on the front. A stairway went up the side of the house, and there was a door at the top. We climbed the porch steps and knocked on the screen door.

A lady with white hair answered.

"Oh, hello, Luther," she said, smiling, "you're just in time for supper." She turned to me. "And who is this?"

"This is Charlie Nebraska," he said. "Charlie, this is Mrs. Hollingsworth."

"Hello," I said.

"Nice to meet you, Charlie." She looked at Luther. "Why don't you take your things up to your room now? Then come down and join the rest of the boarders in the dining room." She slipped a hand into her apron and pulled out two keys.

"Now, Luther," she said, "this key opens the front door and the door at the top of the outside stairs. This other key opens your room. We rarely lock the outside doors, but if we do, you can get in."

"Thank you, ma'am," he said, taking the keys. "I'll

be right down for supper. Charlie, you can come up and take a look at my room if you want to. It's real nice."

I followed Luther up the stairs and down the hall.

He stopped in front of the last room. It had a big brass 3 on the door. He pushed the key into the keyhole and unlocked it.

Just then the door across the hall opened and a short, skinny man walked out. He glanced up at Luther and looked real surprised. "Who're you?" he demanded, like Luther was breaking in or something.

"Luther Peale." He held out his hand. "I'm the new boarder."

The skinny man glared at Luther and didn't shake his hand. "The new *boarder?*" he said. "In *this* house?"

Luther stiffened but nodded. "That's right," he said in a soft voice.

"We'll see about *that,*" the man said. He stormed off to the end of the hall and down the steps.

Luther froze.

"Maybe I shouldn't move in so fast, Charlie," he said. "I might not be stayin'."

"What do you mean?" I asked. "Mrs. Hollingsworth owns this place, right? If she says you can stay, you can stay."

Luther gave a little sigh and stepped into the room. I walked in behind him. He was right. It was a nice place, clean and kind of sunny. A bed was pushed up against the inside wall, and a chest of drawers stood next to the back window.

"Lots of space," Luther murmured, opening the closet door. "Don't have much to hang in it, though." He gazed over his shoulder. "Mrs. Hollingsworth had sinks put in every room." He pointed to the sink next to the closet. A small mirror hung over it. "Bathroom's across the hall."

"How many people live here?" I asked.

"Three other men upstairs here," Luther said. "I take it we just met one of 'em. Mrs. Hollingsworth lives in the rooms downstairs. She makes breakfast and supper for everybody."

I frowned. "I hope you'll still eat with us sometimes. It sure is better than eating with Vern."

"Well, thank you, Charlie," Luther said. "I'd like that."

We put his things away. They only took up one drawer and a few hangers. He took a paper bag out of the gunnysack. He didn't open it but set it on the floor in the back of his closet. I figured it was more of that Tennessee moonshine. But I didn't ask, seeing as how it was none of my business.

"Say, Charlie, would you do me a favor?" Luther asked.

"Sure."

He took out a dollar and handed it to me. "I need some paper to write my daddy and brothers. Could you get me a tablet I could tear paper out of? And some envelopes?"

"Sure," I said. "Woolworth's has that stuff."

"No hurry," he said. "Just when you're over that

way. Now, you better go. I got to go down for supper."

We heard shouting downstairs, and Luther opened the door to the hallway.

"I ain't livin' with a Negro," the voice shouted. "If he's here, I'm movin' *out*."

"Charlie, you better take the outside stairs tonight." I opened my mouth to argue, but he went on. "See if you can get the team to come practice about seven. Over at the diamond where I saw you playing before."

I planted myself in front of him. "Okay, but I'm walkin' downstairs with you."

Luther nodded. "All right, Charlie, but you follow me down."

I walked behind Luther to the end of the hallway and down the stairs. When we got to the bottom of the steps I could see the dining room just past the living room. Two men sat stiff at the table like they had metal rods inside their backs. They stared at their plates.

The third man, the skinny one we saw upstairs, got up. "Mrs. Hollingsworth," he said, pointing his finger at the old lady, "if you let that boy set down here, I'm packin' up and leaving."

Mrs. Hollingsworth, sitting at the head of the table, turned to Luther. Her face was as white as her hair, and her eyes looked scared. She said in a quiet voice, "Mr. Peale, please sit down and join us for supper."

The skinny guy shoved his plate off the table and it crashed to the floor, spilling slices of beef, potatoes, and green beans across the rug. He cussed in a loud voice and stormed into the living room, past us, and up the stairs.

"Mrs. Hollingsworth—" Luther said, his voice hushed.

But she held up her hand. "I never did like him anyway, Luther," she said. "You sit down here and enjoy your supper."

The two men at the table looked uncomfortable, but nodded at Luther. I couldn't believe how calm Luther looked. His insides had to be jumping like mine. He nodded back to them, then turned to me.

"Charlie, I'll see you at the park at seven," Luther said.

"Okay," I said. "See you."

"Nice to meet you, Charlie," Mrs. Hollingsworth said. Her voice was soothing, like she was trying to smooth over what just happened.

"Same here, ma'am," I said.

I walked out the front door, down the sidewalk, and headed toward home.

* * *

I called everybody to tell them about practice. None of them could wait to get coached by a professional baseball player. Even Will said he'd be there. Eileen's voice sounded kind of funny, but she didn't explain why. I found out when I got to the baseball diamond that night.

I could see that something was up when I saw Luther standing at home base looking worried. Parents were piling out of their cars, along with their kids. Eileen's parents were there, along with Walter's and Brian Malone's. They all looked real serious as they walked toward the baseball diamond.

"What's goin' on?" I asked Will.

"Eileen said her dad doesn't like it that Luther's coaching," he said.

"Why?" I asked him. "Because he's colored?"

"I don't know," Will said. "Could just be 'cause he doesn't know Luther."

"But Luther's a professional," I said. "He'll be a great coach! Are they going to let her brothers play?"

Will shrugged.

"Well," I said, "Casey played with the Wildcats, and Coach Hennessey can be mean and boss people around. Besides, Luther's a way better coach."

Will scowled. "Hey, Hennessey's a great coach, Charlie. You shouldn't say all that just because you didn't make the team."

I stared at Will. "Even if I was playin' with the Wildcats, I wouldn't like the way he acts," I told him. I looked over at Luther. "I just want to know why people are suspicious of Luther when he's nice to everybody and he knows so much about baseball."

Will didn't say anything. He just turned and walked away. I didn't have time to think about Will, though, because Mr. McNally walked up to Luther right then.

"We came down here to find out what's going on," Mr. McNally said. "How come you want to coach these kids?"

"They asked me to help," Luther said quietly. His back was straight as a telephone pole, and his words were slow and careful. "I thought maybe I could give them some pointers. Help 'em be better players."

"Where did you come from?" Mrs. Malone asked. "And why did you come here to Holden?"

"I'm from Tennessee, ma'am," Luther said. "Hurt my arm playing ball. I come up north lookin' for work."

"So what's in this for you?" Mrs. Holladay asked, narrowing her eyes a little bit.

I walked over and stood next to Luther. "Nothing's in it for him," I said. "He's a *professional* baseball player, and he's helpin' us. He's my friend, and all of us want Luther to coach us. Right, Eileen?"

"Right," she said, nodding hard.

"Right, Brian?" I asked.

Brian's mom looked at him sharply. He looked uncomfortable and shrugged. "Yeah, I guess so."

"Will?"

Will nodded but looked away.

Mrs. McNally spoke up. "Mr. Peale, some of us were a little uncomfortable because we don't know you—"

"And he's livin' down on the river like a tramp," Mrs. Malone butted in.

"I did spend a couple of nights camping, ma'am," Luther said. "Till I got me a room."

Mrs. Malone still didn't look happy.

I was sorry for Luther because everyone was so suspicious. But I spoke up. "He lives in a boardinghouse over on Willet Street."

Mrs. McNally swatted at a mosquito and said, "Well then." She smiled. "I don't see why Mr. Peale shouldn't teach the kids. Maybe if a parent comes to the practices—"

"I'll come," offered Mr. Malone. His wife looked doubtful, but she didn't say anything.

Walter's dad wiped a hand over his chin. "Well, it's okay with me as long as a parent is here." Walter smiled at him.

Mrs. Malone spoke up. "Johnny O'Toole won't be here. His mother and father won't let him play with a..." Her voice trailed away.

I wanted to say, *His name is Luther Peale,* but something told me to keep my mouth shut.

"Well, my Jim won't be playing, either," said Mrs. Holladay. "Come on, Jim, let's go."

"You said you'd hear what everyone has to say," Jim protested.

"I've heard enough. Let's go." She turned and walked off toward the parking lot. Jim looked at Luther and said quietly, "Sorry."

Luther nodded to him. Jim followed his mom toward the parking lot, but turned back to look over his shoulder. I held up a hand to thank him for trying.

"So, I guess everything's settled, then," Mrs.

McNally said. "Mr. Peale is nice enough to help the kids, and we'll have a parent at every practice." She smiled at Luther. "Thank you, Mr. Peale."

He nodded again and said softly, "Ma'am."

"I'll stay tonight," Mr. Malone offered.

Mrs. Malone turned, shaking her head, and walked to their car. The rest of the parents looked awkward and stared at the ground. A few called out "Thank you" to Luther. Then one by one, except for Mr. Malone, they shuffled off toward the parking lot.

Luther watched them go. His face didn't tell me what he was thinking.

What a day. First Lobo was mean to Luther, then the man at the boardinghouse didn't want him living in the same house with him, and now these parents made him feel bad for trying to help us.

It was kind of a surprise to see some of these people—the parents of my best friends—act so different from how I knew them. Or how I thought they were. It was like you could suddenly see a part of them that they usually kept hidden in the dark.

I felt sorry for Eileen and her brothers. They had to watch their dad act so mean for no reason. I would've been real embarrassed.

But I bet Luther felt a lot worse.

"Sorry about all of that, Luther. But I'm glad we can have our team."

Luther sighed. "Yeah." He looked around at us kids. "Well, I guess we can start practice now."

"Right," I said. "We better get started. We're playing a game in three weeks."

Everyone looked surprised. "We're going to play the Wildcats," I told them.

"*What?*" Bowie yelled.

"Why?" Walter asked, worry spreading over his face.

"It'll give us a goal to work for," Luther said. "We can win this game. We just have to hustle. Hustle wins more games than base hits."

Everyone looked scared except Will. Maybe he was trying to decide which team he'd play on. I was wondering the same thing. He'd be playing "official" games with the Wildcats, but would he play with us against them for *this* game?

"Lobo'll kill us," Walter said. His voice was higher than usual, and his mouth went down so far at the edges I thought he might cry.

"No he won't, Walter," Luther said. "I've seen you kids play ball, and you all have talent. You just need a little coaching and lots of practice. And most of all, you need to believe in yourselves."

"Well, I believe we're gonna get stomped," Kathleen murmured, scratching at a mosquito bite on her leg.

Luther didn't look at her, but he said, "There's no room for negative thinking. You have to believe in yourselves and your teammates. When you're standin' in the batter's box, you *tell* yourself you're going to hit that ball. It don't matter if we have two strikes against us and you're the player we're counting on. You say over and over while you're up at bat, 'I'm gonna hit the ball; I'm gonna hit the ball.' And you keep your eyes on that ball every second. You have to make contact with the ball to put it in play. You *will* hit it."

I could tell my friends were listening hard. They were leaning forward to hear everything Luther said.

"Luther?" Walter put up his hand.

Luther smiled. "You don't have to raise your hand, Walter."

"Are we going to have a team name?" he asked.

Luther's smile widened. "I've been thinkin' about that. How about the Stumptown Stormers?"

"That's good!" I said.

We all said the name to try it out. Everybody liked it.

"Wouldn't it be something if the Stumptown Stormers beat the Wildcats?" Eileen said. "We'd be famous around here!"

I glanced quick at Will. He frowned, but he didn't say anything.

"We'll *never* beat—" Walter stopped himself midsentence. "Uh, no, I mean—"

"Good, Walter," Luther said, nodding. "You caught yourself in negative talk. Keep aware, and stop when you catch yourself talkin' or thinkin' that way. We *can* and *will* beat the Wildcats."

I thought I saw Mr. Malone smile. I wasn't sure

whether he thought that was funny or whether he just agreed with Luther.

"Okay, let's get started," Luther went on. "We're going to work on hitting tonight. Here are some things to remember. It's important to feel comfortable in the batter's box. Wear loose clothes to practice and games. And be sure to keep your body closed while you're at the plate. No 'steppin' in the bucket' to the side. Step *toward* the ball. Now let's see your bats."

Alan brought three bats up to Luther. They were all cracked and taped. Two of them were Louisville Sluggers signed by Stan Musial and Ralph Kiner.

"Okay, these're good," Luther said. "We got any newer bats?"

Nobody said so, and he nodded. "Okay. We'll use these. Everybody line up to bat now. Charlie, you pitch, and remember what I told you about keepin' your fingers across the seams. Follow through. And grab up a pinch of dirt afterward. Use Walter's catcher's pud as a target."

He turned to Walter. "Hold that pud in the middle of the plate about as high as the batter's knee," he said.

First up was Alan. He picked up the Stan Musial bat and got ready.

"Close your stance more," Luther told him. Alan turned slightly to the right. "Now I want to hear you say, 'I'm gonna hit the ball—I'm gonna hit the ball.' Keep sayin' it till your turn's over. And watch that ball. Never take your eyes off it."

Alan's face squeezed up as he focused. "I'm gonna hit the ball," he said. "I'm gonna hit the ball."

Luther nodded at me. I wound up and pitched Alan a good one. He socked it high over my head.

I heard Mr. Malone whistle.

"Excellent!" Luther called out. "Remember the three Cs of hitting: be *comfortable, concentrate,* and make *contact* with that ball. Next up."

It was amazing how much better everybody batted that day. It was almost like Luther worked some kind of magic on us.

I pitched better, too. I only threw two wild ones, and that was because I was thinking about how good we were all doing and I forgot to concentrate.

After everybody had batted awhile, Luther told me to vary my pitches. "Charlie, sometimes aim as high as the batter's left shoulder or as low as the batter's knees," he called out. "Your pitches are much better now, so you don't have to pick up dirt anymore. But be sure you follow all the way through on every pitch."

It was harder, tryin' to aim high and low and in and out. But the more I did it, the better it went.

At the end of practice, Luther gathered everybody around him again.

"Before we come back here tomorrow," he said, "I want you all to practice hitting. Hang up a blanket on your clothesline and hit into it. Don't ever hit a baseball against the backstop or a brick building. It shreds the stitching on it, and you'll ruin it. Use a rubber ball or tennis ball instead."

"Luther?" It was Devin McNally. "We got a coupla balls at home," he said. "But not enough for us all to practice at one time."

Luther thought a second. "You know any farmers?" he asked.

"Yeah," Devin said. "Our grandad has a farm along Highway 218."

"Ask if you can have some corncobs," Luther told him. "Cut 'em in two-inch pieces and soak half of 'em in water for a while. Then dry 'em out for a day or two. Mix 'em with cobs you don't soak and use 'em for pitching and batting practice. See, the dry ones'll float, and the ones that got waterlogged will be heavy. It'll work on the batter's concentration, 'cause he won't know what kind of cob is comin' at him till it leaves the pitcher's hand."

Everyone grinned. I looked over at Mr. Malone. He wasn't the only person watching now. A teacher from the high school who was out for the summer sat on the bleachers, and a lady walking her dog had stopped to watch. I hoped word would get around town that Luther was a great coach. I wanted everybody to be happy he was here. I knew that was impossible with people like Vern and Mr. McNally, but I bet we could win over most of the people in Holden. All they'd have to do is listen to Luther coach us for a while. Then they'd see he was an expert and he just wanted to help us.

Luther worked with us till it was getting dark. Everyone thanked Luther and walked off toward home looking tired and happy. Just before he and Brian left, Mr. Malone went over to speak to Luther.

"You're doin' fine, Luther," he said. "I'm sorry for some of those things that were said tonight. People just have to get to know you, I guess."

Luther nodded.

"It's great the kids can learn from someone of your caliber," Mr. Malone added.

"Thank you, sir," Luther said.

I thought about all the things Luther had taught us tonight. I was beginning to see what he meant about baseball being played mostly in your head. You really did have to believe you could do it and concentrate hard.

I just hoped we could concentrate when we were looking into Lobo's beady eyes and seeing that mean old smirk.

That would take a whole lot of concentration. And we only had three weeks to get ready.

Chapter Ten

I walked down to Woolworth's the next morning to get the writing paper and envelopes for Luther. I put them on the counter next to the cash register where Mom was working.

"What's this, honey?" Mom asked.

"It's for Luther," I said, handing her the dollar. I looked around. Nobody was standing nearby, so I leaned in and whispered, "Mom, could you just call me Charlie?"

Surprise took over her face, and I thought she might laugh. But she clamped her lips together and nodded. "Sure, hon—" She shook her head and smiled. "Sure, Charlie. Sorry. It's a hard habit to break after eleven years, but I'll try to remember."

I nodded.

She looked at the clock. "Say, it's time for my break. Let's get a strawberry lemonade over at the lunch counter."

Mom waved to another clerk who came and took her place at the cash register. I followed Mom to the back of the store. We sat down on round, cushy seats and leaned our elbows on the smooth lunch counter. Mom looked up and said, "Nancy? Two strawberry lemonades, please."

She turned to me. "I've been meaning to ask you—what would you like for your birthday supper? It's coming up fast."

I thought for a minute. "How about hamburgers?" I asked. "Could we cook 'em on the charcoal grill?"

"Sure," Mom said.

"And can Luther come?"

"Oh." Her smile faded. "Well, I—I thought we'd ask Vern to join us. He knows your birthday's on the sixteenth, and he has a present for you."

"I don't want Vern there," I said. "Just Luther."

Nancy came over and set down two icy glasses of lemonade and two straws inside paper wrappers. "Hi, Charlie," she said. Nancy just got engaged a few months ago to the new dentist in town. She likes to flash her diamond ring in people's faces when she hands them their drinks. "I hear you and your friends have a new coach."

"Yeah." Like I said, word travels fast in this town. "I think every person I've seen this morning has had something to say about it."

"Thank you, Nancy," Mom said. I could tell she was hoping that Nancy wouldn't stand there talking to us.

"Me, I just say live and let live," Nancy said.

Mom smiled and nodded but didn't say anything. I

guess Nancy finally took the hint, because she walked away.

We tore the paper off the straws and poked them into our lemonades. I wrapped my hands around the cold glass and took a sip. The sweet drink slid down my throat. I closed my eyes for a second and let the coolness spread through me.

"Charlie." Mom swiveled her seat a little toward me, her face looking troubled. "I hope you can learn to like Vern."

I told her the truth. "I don't see how I'll ever like him. He's about as far away from Dad as anybody can get."

"Honey, you can't compare him to your dad," she said. "There was only one Bill Nebraska."

"But it seems like Vern's always pretending to be somebody he's not."

Mom sipped her lemonade and look at me sideways. "What do you mean?"

"Well," I said, "he pretends he knows a lot about music. And his songs are horrible."

Mom smiled. "They're really something, aren't they? But he loves his music. And he tries so hard."

"He pretends he's a nice guy," I said, "but when he breaks Mrs. Banks's window, he acts like he didn't do it."

"Remember, I told you he said he'd pay for it."

"Only 'cause I told you what he'd done. And most of all, he pretends he's not prejudiced against colored people."

Mom gave out a long sigh and rested her cheek on her hand. "I've got to tell you, Charlie, that disappoints me about Vern. But that's what he was taught growin' up. You learn what your parents teach you."

"That don't make it right," I said.

"Doesn't."

"That doesn't make it right," I said impatiently. "Besides, Vern's all grown up now. He oughta be able to think for himself."

Mom nodded. "You're right."

"How can you like somebody who hates a whole group of people?"

Mom stirred her lemonade with the straw. "Well, I like how Vern's thoughtful." She smiled. "Those flowers he bought me the other day were beautiful. You know, he cares a lot about both of us. He really wants to spend more time with you."

I was in the middle of a sip, so I didn't say anything.

"I do believe that Vern will work his way up in his company because he works so hard. Wouldn't it be good to live in a nicer house? You'd have a grown-up man to do things with, and I'd have company."

This time I opened my mouth, but Mom put up her hand. "Okay, okay. You already told me you don't want to do things with Vern."

She leaned forward again and rested her elbows on the counter. She looked a little sad.

"When he gets to know you better, I bet Vern won't try to pretend so much anymore. He just wants us to love him back, so he tries to be what he thinks we want him to be."

"Except for someone who doesn't care about people's skin color," I said.

Mom sighed again. "Luther's the first colored person we've had living in Holden for a long time. So before Luther came to town, the topic only came up once with Vern and me."

"I just want Luther at my birthday supper," I told her again.

Silence hung between us for a little bit. I heard the store sounds around us—clattering dishes and people's voices, mostly. A baby cried up front near the door. Finally Mom said, "Okay, Charlie. Luther's your special friend, so he should be the one sitting with us at your birthday supper. Maybe Vern can come the next night."

I didn't ever want to have supper with Vern. But at least he wouldn't be there on my birthday to wreck it. "Thanks, Mom."

"I'll just have to think of what I'll tell Vern so he doesn't show up to wish you a happy birthday."

"I think you should tell him the truth," I said. "Tell him I want Luther there, that he's my friend."

Mom stared the table and seemed to be working on something in her mind.

"We'll see. I'll figure something out." She frowned a little. "I guess maybe we both need to get to know Vern better. Before we get marr—" She looked up at me. "Well, before anything, I'll have a long talk with him about Luther. But I don't want to make an issue of it on your birthday. Let's keep that day fun, okay?"

* * *

That afternoon Will and I practiced hitting old rubber balls into the side of Hayes School where there weren't any windows. I was kind of surprised that Will wanted to practice with me. He'd been acting different ever since he got picked for the Wildcats, and I was beginning to think that he didn't want to be my friend anymore. But I saw him when I was walking home from Woolworth's, and we decided to practice.

"Hey, Will," I said, after smacking a good one against the brick building. "Whose side you gonna play on when the Stumptown Stormers play the Wildcats?"

He didn't say anything for a long time. He just hit the ball against the building.

"I gotta play with my team," he said finally.

"The Wildcats?"

"Yeah."

"So why'd you stay at practice with us last night?" I asked him.

Will shrugged. "I don't know."

"I know," I said. "'Cause we're your friends. You're still my best friend, you know." I wasn't really sure if that was true anymore—Luther felt like my best friend now—but I wanted to hear what he'd say.

"Yeah," Will said. But he didn't look at me. And he didn't say I was *his* best friend.

"Do you like Luther?" I asked.

"Yeah."

"You're not prejudiced, are ya?" I asked.

"No."

"So...what's wrong, then?"

"Nothin'," Will said. "Come on, let's practice."

Will had been my best friend since kindergarten. But everything had changed now. It didn't feel the same. I felt like I was practicing with someone I didn't know very well.

We practiced for a while. Then we took a break in the shade of a big oak.

"How come Luther stopped playin' baseball?" Will asked me, settling onto the grass.

"Haven't you noticed his right arm?" I asked. "It don't work very good."

"Yeah," Will said. "How'd he hurt it?"

I wasn't sure what to say. It seemed like Luther had been telling me a secret when he told me about it. But I wanted to show Will I was still friends enough to tell him.

I looked over my shoulder to make sure we were alone. "You swear not to tell this to anybody?"

"I swear." Will's eyes were bright like he knew he was about to hear something important. He edged closer.

So I told him about Luther's game against the white team, and how the batter came up to the plate drunk. "Luther's pitch hit him right in the head and killed him."

"*What?*" Will's eyes were huge now. "Are you *kidding* me?"

I shook my head.

"Man! So Luther's on the run from the law?" Will looked impressed.

"No," I said. "The ump told everybody it wasn't his fault. But the hitter's brother—Ruckus somebody, I think—was going to kill him, so Luther had to get out of town."

"Wow."

"Yeah," I said. "But we can't tell anybody."

"I won't tell," Will promised.

I knew I could count on him. He was still my best friend. Sort of.

We got up and practiced some more and pitched balls to each other, too. I could tell that Will had been listening when Luther reminded me to follow through, all the way to the ground practically. He was practicing the things that Luther taught me. It started working in my mind that Will would take what he learned from Luther and use it against us in the game with the Wildcats.

As I hit the ball, it all got bigger and bigger in my mind. I stopped hitting and looked at Will.

"What?" he asked. "Why'd you stop?"

"I think you should pick," I said, frowning. "The

Wildcats or us. You shouldn't come and learn everything from Luther and then play against us. We're still friends. But if you aren't going to play with us, I just don't think you should practice with us."

Will stared at me a second or two. "Okay," he said. There was an edge to his voice, and his eyes looked dark. "If that's how you feel."

He put down the bat and ball.

"We can still be friends," I said again, softer.

But he turned and walked off across the school yard.

I watched him go. An uneasy feeling lay heavy in the pit of my stomach. I wasn't sorry for what I'd said, though. Will had to choose once and for all.

And he did.

I picked up the ball and bat and headed for home.

* * *

I took the writing pad, the envelopes, and the change from Luther's dollar to Scott Park for baseball practice and left them on the bleacher while we worked that night. Will didn't come. I didn't think he would, but I was hoping he might change his mind and decide to play with the Stumptown Stormers instead.

It was strange not having him there, and I had some mixed-up feelings about it. I hoped that Will was still my friend, but it wasn't fair for him to learn pointers from Luther and then help the Wildcats kill us.

I tried not to think about him too much.

Eileen's dad Mr. McNally came to watch this time, along with three other men who didn't even have kids playing on the Stormers. Mr. Burford, who owned a clothes store downtown, Dr. Pritchard, the new dentist who was engaged to Nancy from the Woolworth's lunch counter, and the third guy who worked at the bank.

I guess most everybody in town had heard about a player from the Negro Leagues coaching us Stormers and they wanted to see what it was all about. Mom said a lot of people were talking about Luther down at the store. Some liked the idea that he was willing to coach us, and some were mad about him teaching white kids. Others thought it was curious that a stranger who just happened to be a professional baseball player had come to Holden, Iowa.

I had a feeling there was going to be a big crowd watching our game against the Wildcats. I figured some would be rooting for us because we were underdogs, and some probably hoped that Luther's team would get creamed. And some others might come just to see how everybody else acted about it.

We concentrated that night on fielding: catching and throwing.

Bowie had tied a softball into his new glove and soaked it and rubbed it with hog lard like Luther told him. He was catching every ball that came near him.

Luther told us that the cardinal rule for the infielders

when a grounder is coming your way is to get that glove all the way down on the ground. Luther said too many balls go right under the glove. And he showed us how to hold the glove up as a shield against the glare of the sun.

"Peek around that glove to see where the ball is," Luther said. He gave us all a chance to catch balls that were coming at us from the west where the sun was edging toward the far trees.

He talked about pitching after that. He had me show everybody what he'd taught me, how to keep your first two fingers over the seams and follow through and pick up dirt or grass after releasing the ball. Everyone worked on that, too.

This was only our second practice, but I could see that we were all getting better already. Like before, it was because of Luther's magic. He just seemed to know the right thing to say to make us better players. Everyone was smiling a lot. Mr. McNally was listening hard to Luther, and I saw him nod once at something Luther said. He still didn't look too happy, though.

I didn't let myself think about Lobo and the game we'd have to play in a little more than two weeks. All I wanted to think about was how much fun it was to work on baseball with Luther and my friends, even though Will wasn't there. After practice, Luther and I ended up walking through the park.

We passed a bench sitting under a tree, and a big hornet came buzzing around Luther.

"Watch your head," I told him. "There's a hornet followin' you."

He swatted at it and another one came out of
nowhere.

"What the..." Luther looked up into the branches of
the tall oak tree. "Well, look there, Charlie," he said.
"A big old hornets' nest."

And there it was, hanging from the second branch,
about ten foot over our heads, looking white and
papery and big as a softball.

"Let's get out of here and not bother 'em," Luther
said.

"Good idea," I said quickly. I'm not much for wasps
or hornets.

We kept walking. "Say, you wanna visit your old
camp at the river for a while?" I asked. We still had
some time before dark, so I knew Mom wouldn't start
to worry yet.

"Okay," Luther said.

People we'd pass would look at us, then put their
heads together and talk some more and look again. If
I knew them, I'd wave. Otherwise I ignored them.

One man waved and called out, "Hi, Charlie. Hi,
Luther."

"You're making us both famous in Holden," I murmured to Luther as I waved back. "I don't even know
who that is."

We turned down Broom Street.

"Luther," I said, "what would you do if you couldn't
stand the man your mom was seein'?"

Luther glanced over at me. "You talkin' about Vern?" he asked.

"Yeah," I said. "I don't like him at all."

"Your mama must see something she likes about him," Luther said.

"She says she might marry him if he asks her."

"And you don't want Vern to be your daddy."

I scowled. "Makes me mad just thinkin' about it. Even if Vern marries Mom, he won't ever be my dad."

Luther nodded and put his hand on the top of my head for a second. "I guess you gotta try and get along with him for your mama."

That surprised me. He'd seen the ugliest part of Vern. How could I get along with someone like that?

We didn't say any more till we got to the river.

Luther's lean-to was still there at the camp. We went down to the edge of the river.

I picked up a stone and tossed it sideways. It bounced across the surface of the water, making a soft slapping sound and then disappearing like an otter diving for fish.

"Four times," I said.

Luther grinned. "That's pretty good. It'll strengthen your pitching arm. Let me try with my left arm." He walked along the bank and found a good, flat rock. He tossed it, and it skipped over the water five times.

"How many skips could you get with your good arm?" I asked him.

"My record was seven," Luther said.

"Once my dad and I were going fishing at Lake McBride and he skipped one *eight* times."

"That's real good," Luther said.

He leaned over and picked through some rocks with the water lapping up over them.

"Whooee," he called out. "Lots o' crawdads here. Charlie, get the jar I left in the lean-to, will you?"

I ran to the lean-to and found the jar sitting on the tree stump.

I grabbed it and ran back to Luther. We put some water in the jar and plopped all the crawfish inside. There were six of them, wiggling their legs around like tiny lobsters.

"Good fishing bait," Luther said, pulling the catfish line out of his pocket. He pulled a piece of cork off the hook, held up the fishing line, and grinned. "Always carry a fishing line with me. Learned that from my daddy. Never know when you'll find a good fishing spot, eh, Charlie?"

"Yeah."

The cork had a slit in it. Luther tied the line around it and through the slit, leaving about a foot of line between the cork and the hook.

"Cork makes a good bobber," he said.

He stuck a crawdad on the hook and threw it into the water. He tied the other end of the line on a stick and poked it deep into the soft dirt next to the river.

He straightened up to look at his line. "That oughta do it," he said.

"My birthday's on the sixteenth," I said.

"That a fact? How old you gonna be?"

"Twelve. Could you come and have supper with me and my mom?"

Luther looked at me. "You ask your mama if it's all right with her?"

"Sure," I said. "And Vern won't be there."

"Well then, I'd be honored, Charlie," Luther said.

He folded his arms over his chest and gazed out at the cork bobber.

"Will you ever have to go back to Tennessee?" I asked him.

"Oh, I guess I'll go back sometime," he said. "I just gotta wait till everything cools down. Maybe till Ruckus Brody stops looking for me."

"But what if he never stops looking?" I asked.

He stared across the water at the trees on the other side. "Well, I don't know, Charlie," he said slowly. "But I sure do miss my family."

Inside my heart I could feel a dividing take place. I wanted Luther to be happy, and that meant he had to go back home to Tennessee. But if he left, I'd lose a good friend.

"I hope you stay in Holden for a long time," I told him.

He smiled. "It's nice havin' a friend here, Charlie," he said.

"When you go back home, you gonna play baseball again?"

"Not if this arm don't work," he said. He walked to the big tree and sat under it.

I sat on the tree stump.

"Tell me some more about playing for the Memphis Mockingbirds," I said.

He crossed one ankle over the other. "Well, they were good times, Charlie. It was hard work, though, and tiring. Lots o' times we played doubleheaders. We'd take a bus to the game in the afternoon. Then we'd get back on the bus and ride to the next town for the second game. 'Course, we couldn't stay in most hotels, so we—"

"How come you couldn't stay in hotels?" I asked him.

"How come? 'Cause white folks didn't want us there," he said, like he was surprised I didn't know.

"Oh." I'd never heard of not letting people stay in hotels. "What's the matter with people like that?"

"A lotta white folks is like that. So sometimes colored folks let us stay in their houses, sleepin' on the floor when they didn't have enough beds. And sometimes we slept in the bus. Coupla times we slept on the floor of a school for colored children. And we couldn't eat in restaurants, neither, so we—"

"You mean white folks didn't let you eat in the restaurants, either?" I could hardly believe it. "Do colored kids go to school with white kids?"

"Not in a lotta places," Luther said.

"These white folks, they're believers?" I asked.

"I s'pose some of 'em are," Luther said. "But that don't mean nothin', Charlie, just because they believe in God. There's white preachers who say the Bible tells 'em not to like colored folks."

"Well," I said, "my dad told me God made everybody even, that nobody's better than anybody else."

"Your daddy was a good man, Charlie," Luther said.

"Yeah. I miss him."

"You keep your daddy here," Luther said, touching his head. "And here." He touched his chest. "And he'll live on forever. You know?"

I nodded.

"You got a real good heart," Luther said.

"You got a good heart, too, Luther," I told him. He smiled.

Being with Luther felt good, like when Dad and I were doing stuff together. Sad feelings about Dad came and sat side by side in my chest along with the happy feelings about Luther. I couldn't figure if I felt like laughing or crying.

So I got up and skipped some more stones across the water.

Luther and I stayed till the sun was nearly down. We didn't catch a fish, but it didn't matter. I don't think Luther minded either. It was just good passing the time together down there by the river.

Chapter Eleven

I kept thinking about one of my Superman comic books. A bad guy figured out how to stop time so he could do lots of crimes, and nobody could stop him because their time was frozen.

I wished I could make time stand still, too, as long as we could all move around. I wanted to go on forever with Luther teaching us about baseball and never have to play that game against Lobo and the Wildcats.

But the time was creeping closer. Every time I thought about it my body went crazy. My stomach flip-flopped, and I got shaky and started sweating. Especially when I heard some of Lobo's friends say Lobo was bragging that he was going to pitch the game against us.

"Anyone can beat those girls," he was saying all over town.

The day before my birthday, I saw Brad Lobo again. It was the first time since Luther had kept him from beating me up.

CAROL GORMAN AND RON J. FINDLEY

Mom and I were shopping at the A&P. I turned down the produce aisle and saw him coming in the door behind his dad and older brother. At first I froze. Then my hands got clammy and my body started to shake. I grabbed a bunch of carrots for Mom and hurried up the aisle, hoping he hadn't see me.

But I guess nothing escapes the beady eyes of Brad Lobo. He followed me around to the aisle with the canned vegetables, then came up behind me and said in a low voice, "Hey, Stumptown. I see you don't have your Negro pal to protect you now. Is that why you have him around? To fight your fights for you?"

I could feel my blood boiling in my ears. "Luther's my friend," I said.

Lobo seemed to see something behind me. He looked startled.

"Brad!" a big voice boomed from behind me. "Let's get out of here. I'm in a hurry."

It was Lobo's dad.

Lobo's face turned red. Then his big brother, who looked like him except bigger, came up behind me. I knew it was him because as he walked past Lobo, he gave him a shove. Lobo called his brother a dirty name, and his brother, who was about sixteen and maybe a hundred sixty pounds, turned and smacked Lobo across the face. The smack sent Lobo into a shelf of canned peas. Lobo slumped to the floor. A couple of cans fell off the shelf, just missing his head.

I hurried to the end of the aisle where their father stood, watching.

He swore loudly and said, "Get your butts over here or I'll come and knock your heads together."

Somehow I believed he'd do it, too. Right there in the canned goods aisle of the A&P.

I found Mom in the dairy section. "What was all that hollering about?" she asked.

"Oh, just a family havin' a squabble," I said, wishing my heart would calm down. "I think they left the store."

I guess I knew then where all Lobo's nastiness came from. Like a dog that's treated bad and gets mean, Brad Lobo probably lived with yelling and smacks in the face all the time. But it didn't make him seem less scary. In fact, I had a feeling I'd better make sure to stay out of Lobo's sight. He was likely to be so embarrassed that I'd seen the way his family treated him, he'd beat me to a pulp next time he saw me.

* * *

The next day it was my birthday. Mom stayed home from work to bake my cake, and she made me leave the house for a few hours after lunch. When I got back, she told me my surprise was in her bedroom and she'd skin me alive if I went in there. So while Mom frosted my cake I sat in the living room and stared at the closed door to her bedroom.

Parents are good at torturing kids sometimes.

Luther came after work at a quarter past five. He handed me a brand-new baseball bat.

"*Wow!* Luther, thanks!"

"I didn't have wrapping paper for it, Charlie," he said. "But happy birthday."

Mom was impressed. "Luther, you didn't need to get Charlie a present. You must have spent a whole day's pay on it."

Luther shrugged. "See, Charlie? It's a Larry Doby bat."

Larry Doby's colored. He plays for Cleveland and boy, can he hit home runs. "This is the best present I ever got." I ran my hand over the smooth, polished wood. "A Larry Doby bat. Thanks, Luther."

Luther grinned. "Glad you like it."

Mrs. Banks was sitting out back in her lawn chair, focusing her crabby eyes on Luther while he helped Mom grill the hamburgers. At first Mom said hello to her and seemed bothered that she was watching us. After about fifteen minutes Mom asked her if she'd like one of the burgers when they were done. Mrs. Banks just frowned and said, "No, thank you," and turned her face away.

We ate inside so we could eat without being stared at.

It was good seeing Luther sitting across the table from me and Mom again.

"How's your job going at Landen's?" Mom asked him.

"Real good, ma'am, real good," Luther said. He smiled and pulled a key out of his shirt pocket. "I got myself another job there. Mr. Landen's payin' me extra to keep the place clean. He gave me my own key today. Mrs. Hollingsworth always has supper ready at five-thirty, so I'll go back at night after baseball practice to do the cleanin'."

"That's wonderful, Luther," Mom said.

Luther told us a funny story about a lady who stood in line for ten minutes to sell her eggs and when she finally got up to the counter, she realized she'd left them at home.

"She was real embarrassed," Luther said, laughing.

I watched him and Mom laughing and talking together. I couldn't help wishing that if Dad didn't come home, Luther could marry Mom and be my dad. If Luther was white, it could happen. I could see that she and him really liked each other. I wondered if it was bad to wish a colored person was white. It sure would've made things easier all the way around.

"And now for your present, Charlie," Mom said after I'd blown out my candles and we'd stuffed ourselves with cake and ice cream. "Luther, I'm going to need your help. Will you come with me? Charlie, you sit in the living room."

We got up from the table, and Luther followed her into her bedroom.

I stood and watched.

After about half a minute Mom and Luther made their way into the living room carrying something big and heavy between them. It was about as tall as my waist, in a heavy wooden cabinet.

I let out a whoop. "It's a television set!"

I'd seen one in the window of Dewey's Furniture, so I knew what it was. People liked to stand on the sidewalk in front of the store and watch the television even though they couldn't hear it. When a ball game was on, there'd be a crowd four people deep watching it.

Mom and Luther set it down for a second. "The man who delivered it said all we have to do is plug it in and adjust the antenna," Mom said. "He showed me how to do it. I hope I remember."

"Here, I'll help," I said. "Where are we gonna put it?"

"Over there," Mom said, nodding at the corner of the room.

We carried it over and set it down.

"Charlie," Mom said, "your dad and I were saving for a television set when he died. I kept saving little by little and finally had enough. And, well, your birthday seemed like a good time to get it."

"Thanks, Mom!" I said. "I never thought we'd have one."

I only knew a few kids who had a television set, and none of them were good friends of mine. Most folks in Stumptown couldn't afford one. I couldn't believe Mom really bought it for us.

"Here's where you turn it on," she said.

She twisted the knob. First came a sizzling sound, then voices.

A dot of light in the middle of the screen grew bigger and bigger and became a black-and-white picture. A funny-looking man with a bushy mustache and glasses and wearing a bow tie stood there looking out at a laughing audience we couldn't see.

He held up a cigar he was smoking and asked, "Who was the second president of the United States?"

"That's Groucho Marx," Mom said.

"The second president?" I asked. "I never heard of him."

Mom laughed. "No. That man on TV is Groucho Marx." Her smile faded a little. "When I was little I loved the movies he made with his crazy brothers."

I guess they were playing a game on TV. A man and a lady had to answer the questions Groucho asked them.

Mom couldn't take her eyes away from the picture.

"Isn't it amazing?" she said. "These people are maybe 2,000 miles away in California, and we're watching them right here in Holden, Iowa."

Luther shook his head. "Can't hardly imagine it."

Mom and I sat back on the davenport and Luther took the rocking chair. We watched for nearly an hour.

After that show we watched a program on a different channel. It was a story, like a movie. I heard crunching gravel outside. I leaned to the side to look out the window.

"Mom," I said, my pulse suddenly charging, "didn't you tell Vern not to come tonight?"

"Oh no," she said, getting up to look out the window. "I told him we'd celebrate *tomorrow* night."

"I have to leave, anyway," Luther said. He sprang to his feet. "Thank you, Mrs. Neb—"

"*No!*" I shouted so loud Mom and Luther stopped and looked at me. "This is *my* birthday, and this is *our* house, Mom. Don't let Vern chase Luther off. It isn't fair!"

"Oh no, Charlie," Luther said. "I really do have to be goin'."

Mom stared at me a second. "No, you're right, Charlie. This has been a nice night. Luther, you just sit down again. Besides, this television show isn't over yet."

Luther's mouth got tight, and he sat back down in the rocking chair. He looked miserable. I felt bad for making him stay to make a point with Vern, but I was sick of Vern telling us what was what.

Mom went to the door. "Vern," she said, "this is a nice surprise, but like I told you, Charlie wanted to have one of his friends spend the evening on his birthday."

Vern yanked the door open, stalked into the living room, and stopped in front of Luther.

His voice was low and calm, but his face was red. "I thought this might be the friend Charlie invited."

"Go home, Vern," I said.

"Charlie, keep quiet," Mom said. "Vern, please. This is Charlie's birthday. Let's not spoil the day."

"Mary, I'm askin' you nice to tell this...fella...to go home now," Vern said. "We need to talk."

"No, Vern," Mom said. She went over and put a hand on Vern's arm. "I won't do that. We can talk later. Luther is Charlie's friend, and...he's my friend, too."

Vern's mouth dropped open.

"I think you better leave now, Vern," Mom said.

"*I* better leave?" Vern hollered. "Mary, I swear, if I walk out that door now, I'm not coming back."

"Go, Vern," I said.

"Charlie, you hush up!" Mom cried.

Vern turned and stomped across the living room and out the door. Mom, Luther, and I froze like statues while his car roared to life, crunched back out of the driveway, and took off down the street.

"Well." Mom was the first of us to come to life. Her voice was trembling. "I'm sorry that happened. Real sorry. Excuse me."

She blinked a few times, then went into her bedroom and closed the door.

Luther stood up, his face sad. "I gotta go, Charlie. It was a nice party. You tell your mama I said thank you."

"I'm sorry, Luther," I said. "I hope he never comes back. Ever."

Luther patted my shoulder and left.

I sat in the living room and stared at Mom's bedroom door, with a dull ache throbbing in my chest.

* * *

I sat in front of the television set for an hour, looking at the screen but not really seeing it. All I could think of was how upset Mom was and how sad Luther was and how Vern had ruined my birthday.

I missed Dad so bad. Everything had been all mixed up since he left for the war.

Vern had made Mom happy again. But now she was back in her bedroom with the door shut, like two years ago. And it was all my fault.

No, it wasn't. It was *Vern's* fault. He shouldn't have come tonight when he wasn't invited. He's prejudiced and mean, and he wrecked my birthday.

When Mom finally came out, her eyes were red and swelled up, and her hair was messy.

"Charlie, honey, I'm sorry about what happened," she said, touching her hair. She smiled a little. "It was a nice celebration till the end, wasn't it?"

"Yeah."

She sat on the davenport and put her arm around me. I leaned my head on her shoulder.

"I just need some time to adjust a little," she said. "Seems like things happen sometimes, and we've got to get ourselves back on our feet before we can move again."

I squeezed her hand. She sniffled a few times and said in a soft voice, "I sure do miss your dad."

The audience on the TV was laughing, but Mom and I just sat there and stared at the screen.

Chapter Twelve

The Stumptown Stormers practiced after supper every night. A lot of the parents and people from town had started coming to our workouts. Sometimes there were twenty-five or thirty people in the stands. Most seemed interested in hearing what Luther had to say, smiling and clapping when we did well. A few people just sat there and watched.

I wasn't concentrating too good. Mom had been pretty quiet ever since my birthday supper. I was glad Vern wasn't coming over anymore, but I kept wondering how long it would take before she would be happy again. She was talking a lot more about Dad. She'd say what a good man he was, and then she'd tell me the story again of how he saved his friend's life, as if she hadn't told me fifty times already. One time I saw her take his picture down from the wall to look at it closer. He was wearing his Army uniform, and he smiled into the camera. Her eyes got tears in them, and she dusted off the frame with her apron and hung it back up.

I wished I could hear her laugh again.

If Dad could come home, we'd be happy. I bet Dad would even help Luther coach our team.

That Friday night Luther was working us hard. This was our last practice before the game against Lobo's team, and it was like he was trying to squeeze in every bit of coaching he could.

I threw some wild pitches. Luther finally came up and said in a quiet voice, "You're not thinkin' about what you're doin' this week, Charlie." His eyes had a worried look. "How's your mama?"

"She's still sad."

He nodded. "You want to take a walk later?" he asked.

"Yeah," I said.

I tried to keep my mind on the practice after that.

"When the ball's in motion," Luther kept calling out, "no one stands still. Anticipate where the ball's going."

"Follow through on those pitches," he hollered.

"Touch the *inside* of those bases if you're going for the extra base," he yelled.

"Everyone has a job to do," he shouted.

"Hustle, hustle, hustle!"

He stopped us once to practice bunting, which he called a "high art."

"Turn toward the pitcher," Luther said. "Slide your top hand about three-quarters of the way up the bat and pinch the back of it. Don't strike at the ball when you're bunting. Even major leaguers make that mistake. It should feel like you're catchin' the ball with the bat. When the ball comes in contact with your bat, it should be almost at arm's length away from your body. And keep remindin' yourself: *Watch that ball.*"

He also showed us the drag bunt. It's a surprise bunt, where the hitter stands as if he's going to swing but suddenly turns to touch the ball with the end of the bat and immediately takes off running.

We practiced bunting both ways for a while till everyone seemed to get the hang of it.

When practice was almost over, Luther talked about sliding.

"You have a better chance of being safe if you slide," he said. "So always slide if it's a close play. It's almost never too early to start your slide. Even eight feet away, you can start it. Ballplayers break their legs when they start sliding too late."

He sat on the ground and showed us what our legs should look like in a straight slide, with the top leg straight and the bottom leg bent with that ankle tucked under the knee of the straight leg.

"So you slide in on that bent leg and your backside," Luther said. "But if you're running to second or third or home, and it looks like you might get tagged, watch what's goin' on. If the baseman's goin' to tag you, say, on the outside of the base, use a hook slide to the inside of the base. That's like this."

Luther made one leg straight and bent the other at

the knee like the letter *L*. "And you touch the inside corner of the base with the toe of your bent leg," he said.

"If you're goin' to get tagged on the inside of the base, you use the hook slide to the outside. Everybody get that?"

Heads bobbed up and down.

"A good way to practice sliding," Luther went on, "is off a slide on the playground. You know those wax paper bags your bread comes in? Sit on those, and you'll rip down the slide like greased lightnin'. When your body shoots off the slide at the bottom, get your legs in position and slide in. Okay? Everybody practice that before tomorrow."

We all nodded and started to leave. "The game starts at two," Luther called after us. "Be there one hour before the game."

Everyone smiled, but I could tell they were nervous. They wanted to win the game real bad, but I don't think anybody believed we could do it. We mostly just didn't want to get killed.

Just then Mr. McNally came running from the parking lot, shouting. Mrs. McNally was right behind him, and she looked real worried. Everyone turned to see what was going on.

"Don't anybody leave!" he shouted. "I got some news about this man who's coaching our kids. You're going to want to hear it."

People stopped where they were. Luther frowned.

His back was stiff, and he seemed to be watching everybody at once.

Mr. McNally stopped right in front of Luther. "I found out why Luther Peale is here in Holden!" he hollered. Everybody moved in closer to hear. "He had a reason for running from Tennessee, all right."

"Well, out with it, Alvin," Mr. Malone said. "What've you got?"

Mr. McNally waited a second or two more, like he wanted to stretch out the suspense as long as possible. "You folks didn't mind that he was coaching our kids. Well, you're going to change your minds fast. Because he's a *murderer.*"

Luther froze to the spot where he was standing next to the batter's cage. Everyone started talking at once. Finally Mr. Malone hollered to everyone to hush up.

"What are you talking about, Alvin?" he demanded.

Mr. McNally crossed his arms. "Seems he killed a man—a white man—down South," he said, sounding real satisfied. "He ran off and ended up here, coaching our kids."

Murmurs ran through the crowd. Even the kids were looking at each other and talking.

"Now, how do you know that, Alvin?" Kathleen's mom shouted above the crowd. Everyone quieted to listen.

"My wife heard it," Mr. McNally said, jerking his head toward her. Mrs. McNally put a hand over her mouth and looked at the ground. I couldn't tell whether she was upset because of what she'd heard about Luther or because her husband was acting this way.

Mr. McNally went on. "I thought she was actin' funny, and she finally came out with it. Our nephew heard it from Will Draft."

My whole body went numb. Will *told!* How could he do that to Luther? Then I realized I'd done the same thing. Will wouldn't have known if I hadn't told him. I never felt so awful. Ever.

Mr. Malone turned to Luther, his face looking hard, like a piece of granite. "What do you say about all this, Luther?"

Luther unfroze himself and took a step forward. "What Mr. McNally says is true, sir. A man died, like he says."

"What?" Eileen cried. Her face squinched up like she couldn't believe it.

"You *killed* somebody?" Walter asked. He looked like he might start bawling.

"Tell the rest," I told Luther. "Tell them how it was an accident!"

"You knew about this, Charlie?" Mr. McNally shot me an angry look. "And you didn't tell anyone?"

"Let Luther tell what happened," Mr. Malone said.

Luther looked around at all the shocked faces. "It was an accident. I was pitchin' an exhibition game with a white team. The batter had been drinkin' a lot. I threw a pitch, a good one. But his shoulders were slumped over, and his head was hanging. And the ball hit him in the head. I never meant to hurt him."

"If it was an accident, why'd you run?" Mrs. Malone snapped.

"Sheriff told me I oughta get out of town till the batter's brother settled down," Luther said. "He was tellin' people he was going to kill me."

"Well, you sure didn't tell any of us about that, did you, boy?" Mr. McNally said. "You just said you hurt your arm and came up here looking for work."

Luther stared at the ground and didn't answer.

"How do we know he's telling the truth now? Huh?" Mr. McNally shouted, looking over the crowd. He probably wanted to find someone to help him with all the yelling.

"Simple thing, Alvin," Mr. Pink said with a calm voice. "We'll have the sheriff check out his story. See if it's true."

"Okay, fine. Let's take him down to the sheriff ourselves, right now," Mr. McNally said. "Otherwise he'll leave town, like he did after the murder."

"Stop saying *murder*," I cried. "It was an *accident!*"

But nobody heard me this time. Everybody was talking, and Mr. Malone was guiding Luther toward his car. He said something to Mrs. Malone, waving her off and curling his finger at some of the other men to come with him and Luther.

"You goin' to the sheriff's office?" I asked Dr. Pritchard, who was standing next to me.

He nodded. "But Charlie, I think you'd better leave this to the adults," he said.

"But I need to go. Luther's my friend," I told him. "He was helping me with baseball before we ever had a team."

I didn't tell him that this whole thing was my fault because I opened my big mouth to Will.

Dr. Pritchard gazed off a second or two. "Well, okay, Charlie," he said. "But if the sheriff asks you to leave, you'll have to go."

"Okay," I said.

We walked to the parking lot. I climbed into Dr. Pritchard's car and we rode down to the sheriff's office. There was a whole line of people, maybe a dozen cars, heading toward the same place.

"What does your mom think of Luther coaching you kids?" Dr. Pritchard asked.

"She likes him a lot," I said. "We had him over for supper a couple times."

Dr. Pritchard nodded. "I was impressed at practice tonight. Looks like he's taught you and your friends some important skills." He looked over at me. I guess I must have looked nervous because he said, "We'll get to the bottom of this. Nobody will hurt Luther, you don't need to worry about that."

I just nodded and sat there, my stomach hurting because of what I'd done. Poor Luther.

Dr. Pritchard parked, and we got out of the car.

"Thanks for the ride, Dr. Pritchard," I said. "If you don't mind, I'm going to go on ahead."

I ran toward the sheriff's office a half block away. I had to run around the people already heading up the walk.

"He should be run out of town for not telling us," Mr. Roberts from the hardware store was saying as I passed.

But he did tell someone. He told me. And I let him down.

"Well, he sure knows his baseball," someone else farther ahead in the line said. "I never saw anyone who can coach these kids like Luther can."

I climbed up the stairs to the sheriff's office and pushed my way inside.

Mr. and Mrs. McNally, Mr. and Mrs. Malone, Mr. Pink, Luther, and a whole lot of other people had crowded into the office. It was a small room with hardwood floors, two desks, and a bunch of file cabinets.

The deputy's name was on his name tag. Don Mead. He looked like he didn't know what to do with all these people pushing their way into the office. "What's going on here?" he asked.

"We want information on the Negro," Mr. McNally said.

"His name is *Luther*," I said in a loud voice.

Mr. McNally glanced at me sharply and back at the deputy. "We want to know what happened down in Tennessee."

Sheriff Engle opened a door to his office and walked out, frowning.

Mr. McNally kept on talking. "He killed a white man, and we heard his story. Now we want to know if he's tellin' us the truth."

"You asking about Luther Peale?" the sheriff asked.

"We're checking out his story," Mr. McNally said.

Sheriff Engle nodded. "I paid Mr. Peale a visit at his campsite on the river when he first came to town. And I checked him out."

"It was an accident, wasn't it?" Mr. Malone asked.

"According to the sheriff I got hold of in Tennessee," the sheriff said, "Mr. Peale threw a pitch that hit a batter in the head and killed him. Umpire and everyone else said it was a good pitch. The batter was drunk and hangin' his head. It wasn't Mr. Peale's fault."

"Well," Mr. McNally said, "even if it was an accident, he should've told us about it."

"And you would've acted like you're acting now," Mr. Pink said.

Mr. McNally turned red and scowled at the wall.

I let out a breath and peered at Luther through the crowd. Now he was safe. He looked calm, but he was listening to the talk around him.

"Seems that Mr. Peale's brother took a beating from the batter's brother that was meant for him," the sheriff went on.

Luther's head jerked up. "What?" he said.

"You have a brother named Amos?" the sheriff asked.

"Yes." His eyes were blazing.

"Seems Ruckus Brody, the brother of that batter who died, mistook your brother for you," Sheriff Engle said. "Amos is gonna make it, but he was beat up pretty bad." He watched Luther's face, and he cleared his throat. "I'm sorry to have to tell you that."

Luther's eyes burned fire and he worked his jaw so the muscles were popping all over the place. Everyone in the room was quiet.

Mr. Pink cleared his throat. "Well, it looks like we can all go home now," he said. "Thank you, Sheriff."

"But make no mistake," Mr. McNally said, his finger in Luther's face as he left, "we'll be watching you. And after the game tomorrow, I'm pullin' my kids off the team."

"Oh now, Alvin," Mrs. McNally protested.

"I think we ought to thank Luther for giving Holden's children the benefit of his expertise," Dr. Pritchard said.

Mr. Roberts grumbled something under his breath on his way out of the office.

"You want a ride home, Luther?" Mr. Pink asked.

"I'd rather walk, thank you," Luther said. His voice sounded tight like he was trying to keep control. He turned toward the door.

I walked up beside him. "Can I come with you?" I asked.

"Charlie, I think you should go on home," he said.

"Can I at least walk you to the boardinghouse?"

He nodded, and we walked out the door.

People followed us for a few blocks. They were talking about Luther, loud enough for him to hear. Some defended him, and other people seemed disappointed that he wasn't a murderer.

"Come on," I said, turning down a side street. "This won't get you home sooner, but we'll lose those people who're followin' us."

The guilt I was carrying around with me was getting heavier and heavier.

"Luther," I said, "what happened just now—"

"It's over, Charlie," Luther said. His voice was flat. "But I've made up my mind. I got to get home. Amos took a beating for me, and I got to see him. And have it out with this Ruckus fella. This town isn't good for me anyway."

How was I going to tell Luther what I did? What if he hated me? The guilt and the shame were boiling up inside of me now. I couldn't just pretend that it didn't happen. If I didn't say anything, there wouldn't be much difference between me and Vern when he busted Mrs. Banks's window.

I looked up at Luther. A voice inside my head screamed, *Say it!*

I took a breath and said it fast. "Luther, this whole thing was my fault."

Luther frowned and looked at me. "Why's it your fault?"

I blinked hard to keep the tears inside my eyes. "I

told Will Draft about why you came up here from Tennessee. That's how everybody knows. I shouldn'ta told him. I—I'm sorry. I'm real, real sorry."

Luther didn't say anything for a while. I felt better because I'd said it and the boiling in my chest was simmering down. But I wanted to know what he was thinking, if he hated me now. His face didn't tell me.

"Charlie," he finally said. His words came out slow. "This is *my* problem. If I'd told everybody the whole story right away, none of this would've happened."

I wanted to believe him, but I wasn't sure I did. "I bet Mr. McNally would still have acted like he did," I said. "Because you're colored."

Luther was quiet again for a bit. "Charlie, you're still a boy. Your daddy died, but no one put you in charge of fixin' the world's problems. You shouldn't have to worry about grown-up things yet. Your mama can take care of herself, and so can I."

He patted my shoulder. "You didn't do nothin' wrong. But I got to go home. Tomorrow, after the game."

At least he wasn't mad. But even so, I walked alongside Luther feeling sick. Everything was messed up now. My mom was sad. Will wasn't my friend anymore. Everybody felt different about Luther, and they seemed mad at each other, too. We were probably going to get killed by the Wildcats tomorrow. And now Luther was leaving.

It couldn't get any worse.

We got to the boardinghouse and walked up the outside stairs. Luther was about to open the door to his room when another door opened down the hall. A tall man with glasses poked his head out.

"Oh, Luther," he said. "Mrs. Hollingsworth gave me one of your letters by mistake."

"Thanks, John," Luther said. He took a few long strides down the hall and took the white envelope. He looked at it. "From my brother George."

The man went back into his room. Luther came to his door, turned the key in the lock, and we went inside. "He's probably tellin' me about Amos." Luther ripped the envelope open and quickly read the letter.

He frowned and swallowed.

"What's the matter?" I asked.

He didn't seem to hear me. He sank into a chair next to the window and sat, his body stiff. I think he was reading the letter again. When he finished, he pulled a bandanna out of his pocket and patted his forehead.

I was getting nervous again. What did the letter say?

"You okay, Luther?" I asked him. I was still standing in the middle of the room. "What's wrong?"

"Seems Ruckus Brody's comin' up here to Holden," Luther said.

"Oh no." I started breathing fast. "He said he'd kill you."

"Yes, he did."

Panic spread through me like fire through dry timber. "But how'd he know where you were?" I asked him.

"Seems Ruckus has a friend in the post office," Luther said. "When my daddy got my letter, the fella saw my address and gave it to Ruckus. Ruckus told him he's headin' up to Iowa."

"Luther, you got to get out of here!" I said.

Luther slowly shook his head. "No, Charlie. Not this time. Like I said, I'm gonna face Ruckus Brody."

"But he's gonna *kill* you, Luther," I cried. "You can't stay around here." The back of my throat burned, and I could feel tears about to come again. I blinked over and over, trying to hold them back. "Please don't die, Luther. It was real bad when everybody said my dad died. I don't want you to die too. Please go away!"

Luther got up and put his hands on my shoulders. "Don't you worry, Charlie. Like I said, this is a grown man's trouble. It's not for you to take on."

I shoved Luther away. "You told me there wasn't nothin' wrong with walkin' away from a fight! You told me fighting never solved nothin', remember?"

"I know," Luther said. "But Charlie, this is different. What kind of life do I got if I keep running? I shouldn't have left in the first place. My brother took a beating meant for me. I need to get this settled so I can go back home and live near my family."

"Maybe it'll be just your dead body that goes back home," I told him. "Like my dad."

"Sometimes a man's got to stand up for himself," Luther said. "And this is one of those times, Charlie."

"So what are you gonna do?" I asked him. "Sit around like a duck, waitin' to get blasted out of the water?"

"I'm going to be careful, Charlie, that's what," Luther said. "Go about my business, but I'll be watchin' my back."

"You got a gun?" I asked him.

"Of course not," he said.

"You got a knife?"

He shrugged. "A pocketknife."

"That's no good," I told him.

"And what makes you the expert on weapons?" Luther asked, frowning.

"Well, I'm no expert," I said. "But you gotta have a weapon for protection."

"I'll think about it." He didn't look at me when he said it.

I had to think of something, but it was like my head was spinning with questions. When would Ruckus get here? How could I make Luther see that he had to protect himself? How could I help him? How could I make sure he didn't die?

I didn't know what I'd do. But I had to do something.

By the time Luther was finished thinking about it, he might be dead.

Chapter Thirteen

After my dad died, a friend of his in Korea sent us his bayonet. It's the long knife that fits on the muzzle of Dad's rifle. Mom keeps it in the back of the hall closet.

She never lets me hold it unless she's with me. She says she's worried about an accident. But I don't know what kind of accident I could have, unless I was running and playing war or something.

I knew Mom would never let me give the bayonet to Luther. Not because she wouldn't want Luther to have it, I bet, but because she wouldn't let me carry it over to him. And if I asked her to come with me to give Luther the bayonet, she'd want to know why. And then I'd have to tell her about Luther killing that white ballplayer, and she might think different of him. I didn't want to take that chance. I knew she'd hear about it soon—the story would be all over town within a day or so—but I had to get the bayonet to Luther *now*. It might save his life.

My plan was to sneak into the house, get the bayonet out of the closet, and take it back to Luther without Mom knowing. It might be hard, but I had to do it somehow.

It was still light outside, but the sun was sinking. The shadows stretched long across the front yard as I came up to our house from the side. Mom had been spending a lot of time in her room lately with the door closed. If she was there now, that would work out good. I could pull open the closet door, take the bayonet, and be gone without her even knowing I'd been in the house.

But if she was in the living room watching the television set, I'd have to sneak in the back door. It would be real hard to get to the closet, open it, get the knife, and leave without drawing her attention. All she'd have to do was turn and look back over her shoulder and she'd see me.

I thought maybe I should wait till she was asleep. But then I thought if Ruckus was on his way north to kill Luther, there was no telling how soon he could get here. I had to get Luther the bayonet right away so he could protect himself.

I sneaked up to the side window of the living room and peeked in.

Mom was sitting on the davenport, watching the television set.

Uh oh.

This was going to be hard.

I walked real careful around back, trying not to step on any sticks or leaves, and walked as soft as I could into the kitchen through the back door.

A man on the television was acting silly and dressed up like a lady. Mom was laughing. That surprised me, but I was glad. For one thing, she must be feeling better. And for another, if she was laughing, she'd be less likely to hear me behind her.

I stepped into the living room and crept across the hardwood floor behind her. I stopped at the closet in the hallway.

My heart was pounding hard. I reached out and wrapped my hand around the closet doorknob. I twisted it slowly, keeping one eye on Mom and praying the hinges wouldn't squeak when I opened the door.

The audience on the television laughed hard then, so I pulled it open. The hinges squeaked a tiny bit, but Mom laughed again, leaning forward.

She didn't hear it.

I reached into the closet and felt under a pile of folded sheets on the middle shelf. My hand closed around the bayonet's leather case, and I pulled it out.

But just then the man on the television disappeared and a commercial came on. Mom turned her head and jumped a little.

"Charlie, you startled me!" she said. "I didn't know you were home." She got up and came over to me. "What are you doing with your dad's bayonet?"

My shoulders started to sag, but I pulled myself up. I had to tell her the truth now. She had to listen to me and help Luther.

"Mom, I have to take Dad's bayonet to Luther," I said. "I promise I won't take it out of the case."

"Absolutely not, Charlie. You know how I feel about—"

"But he has to have it," I begged.

Mom frowned. "And shame on you for trying to sneak in here and get it."

"Mom," I said. "Please. Luther's in danger."

"What? Whatever for?" Now she looked worried. That wasn't a good sign.

"A man from Tennessee is comin' up here to kill him," I said. "Please, Mom, he needs to protect himself."

"Wait. Wait just a minute." I could see fear edging into Mom's face. *"Why* is a man coming to kill Luther?"

"Sheriff Engle knows all about it," I said, talking fast. "See, Luther accidentally killed a man—" Mom gasped and put her fingertips on her mouth. I started talking *real* fast. "It wasn't his fault, Mom! Ask Sheriff Engle. Luther was pitchin' a game against a white team down in Tennessee, and the batter was drunk, and Luther's fastball—it was a good pitch, the ump said so—it hit the batter in the head, and he died. So the batter's brother who hates colored people is comin' up here to find Luther. We *have* to give him

Dad's bayonet, Mom. It's the only way he can protect himself."

The bathroom door had been closed all this time, and I hadn't even noticed. But now it flew open behind me and Vern came charging out. "What'd I tell you, Mary?" he hollered. His face was red and he waved one arm around his head like he was a crazy person. "This—this coach who Charlie says is so wonderful has *killed* somebody. I told you no good would come of this!"

"What're *you* doin' here?" I couldn't believe that Mom had let Vern back into our lives. And he'd been waiting in the bathroom, listening to everything we said. I got madder and madder.

"Calm down, Charlie," Mom said, putting up her hands. "Vern came here to make up."

"Tell him to get out of our house!"

"Charlie, lower your voice," Mom said firmly. "He came to apologize for what he said about Luther."

"Well, obviously I was right about him!" Vern shouted. "Now we find out he's a *murderer.*"

"Will you two just calm down," Mom said. Her voice was shaking. "Let's sit down and straighten this out—"

"It was an accident!" I cried. "Didn't you hear what I said?"

"Charlie," Mom said, "how could you know this about Luther and not tell me?"

"Listen, Mom!" I yelled. "You're not listening. It

wasn't Luther's fault! I told you, you can ask Sheriff Engle."

"So why did he come up North then, Charlie?" Vern asked. "You explain that to your mother and me."

"I don't have to explain nothing to you, Vern!" I screamed. "I *hate* you!"

"Charlie!" Mom's voice was loud and angry. "Don't you talk like—Give me the bayonet." She held out her hand. *"Now."*

Rage boiled up inside of me. I wanted to jump on Vern and hit him and kick him. But I didn't do that. Instead I did something even worse. I started bawling like a little kid.

"What's Luther going to do?" I cried. I shoved the bayonet case toward Mom. She took it and slapped it on the hall table.

"I'll take that," Vern said, and scooped it up.

Seeing Vern holding my dad's bayonet set off something that felt like a bomb inside me. My chest vibrated with every slam of my heart.

"Luther will just have to take care of himself," Mom said. "I'm sorry about what happened to him. But if Vern is a big enough man to admit he was wrong, I think we should give him a chance to show us—"

"Vern just told you what you wanted to hear."

"Why, I ought to put you over my knee!" Vern hollered.

Mom whirled on Vern. "Vern, you better leave. Right now."

"Mom," I pleaded. "I gotta help Luther. I don't want him to die. We can't let him die."

"Oh, Charlie," Mom said, wrapping her arms around me. "You miss your father so much. So do I, honey. But you can't protect Luther. You're just a little boy, and—"

I shoved her as hard as I could, a new feeling of rage roaring through me.

"I'm not a little boy!" I shouted. "I'm Luther's friend. And he needs me! Maybe you don't have to help him. But I *do*."

I turned to look again at my dad's bayonet in Vern's hands and I didn't even think about it. I ripped it right out of his hands and ran past him and Mom, through the living room and kitchen and out the back door.

"Charlie!" Mom cried behind me. "Come back here! Come back here right now!"

But I kept running as fast and as hard as I could toward Luther's boardinghouse.

Chapter Fourteen

I was afraid Mom and Vern would come after me in the car, so I ran through backyards and alleys as much as I could. I was still clutching the bayonet in its case, and it was heavier than it looked. My chest started aching after the first three blocks, but I kept running.

I'd told Mom about Luther's boardinghouse, and she said she knew the place. She'd probably left home in the car by now. I just had to get there before she and Vern did.

And Luther had to take the bayonet.

I knew I'd be in big trouble whenever Mom caught up with me or when I went home, but that didn't matter now. Luther needed me, and I was going to help him.

It was starting to get dark. A big, orange sun crouched behind the trees as I ran, pitching long shadows across the street. In a few minutes it would disappear, and the night would throw a curtain over everything. Including Ruckus, if he was in town already.

I ran even faster.

Finally the boardinghouse came into sight. Lights were on inside, but Luther's window was dark. Where was he? Maybe he'd gone to Landen's to clean up.

I had to be sure he wasn't in his room.

I ran up the outside stairs, pulled open the door at the top, and hurried to Luther's room.

"Luther!" I called, knocking loud. "Luther!"

I heard footsteps on the stairs at the far end of the hall. I stuck the case with the bayonet behind my back, in case it wasn't Luther.

Mrs. Hollingsworth came up, towels hanging over her arm.

"Well, hello," she said, smiling. "You're Charlie, right? Luther's friend? My, but he's popular tonight."

"He isn't here?" I asked breathlessly.

"No, honey," she said. "He went back to Landen's to do some cleaning, I think."

I stood there, breathing hard. Now I'd have to run to Landen's. If I went home without giving Luther the bayonet, Mom would take it away and not let me give it to him.

Then something Mrs. Hollingsworth had said wormed its way into my mind. "What'd you say about Luther bein' popular?" I asked.

"Oh, a fella was just here, inquiring for Luther. Not even five minutes ago."

My heart stopped for a second. "Was he from Holden?"

"No," Mrs. Hollingsworth said. "He had a lovely Southern accent."

A sound like a cry escaped from my throat.

"Said he'd just come up from Tennessee." She frowned. "What's wrong, dear? You look like you've seen a ghost."

My heart was thrashing now. "Did you tell him where Luther was?"

"Well, sure I did," Mrs. Hollingsworth answered, still frowning. "And I gave him directions, too. I don't think he had a car, though. He must've come up here on the train. Why, what's the matter?"

"Call the sheriff, Mrs. Hollingsworth!" I backed away. "Tell him a man named Ruckus Brody is after Luther. Tell him to go to Landen's!"

"Charlie, wait," she called after me. "I don't understand."

But I was already out the door and running down the outside stairs.

Chapter Fifteen

At the bottom of the stairs, I saw Mom's car pull up at the curb. I ran behind the boardinghouse and a hedgerow that stood between me and the car.

Then I headed down the street, running as fast as I could. My chest ached something awful. I was pretty near crying, to tell the truth, knowing that my dad's bayonet might be the only thing that could keep Luther alive tonight.

I *had* to get it to him before Ruckus found him.

The sun had set, and darkness was swallowing up Holden as I tore along the streets. Maybe the dark would slow Ruckus down. Maybe he'd have a hard time finding Landen's, and I could get there first. Mrs. Hollingsworth said it was less than five minutes ago that she saw him.

I wondered if I might even pass him on the way.

Let me get there first, I said to God or Dad or anyone who might be able to help. *Just let me get there ahead of Ruckus.* I added a *please* in case good manners counted when you made requests like that.

It probably took ten minutes to run to Landen's, but it seemed more like an hour. When I was a block away, I saw the lights shining from the windows like they were looking for me and calling me to hurry.

I hoped Luther had locked the doors behind him. Nobody locks their doors in Holden. But I hoped Luther was in the habit of putting on locks. Maybe they locked up their houses in Tennessee.

I raced up the street, and just as I got close, I saw him. A man was outside Landen's, crouched deep in the shadows at a side window near the front. He was peeking inside.

Ruckus Brody. It had to be him.

I ran up on the stoop, threw open the screen, and pushed through the big door. The front room was empty. "Luther!" I called out. I had my fingers on the lock and was closing the door behind me when Ruckus shouldered the door and heaved it open, pushing me out of the way.

"Where is he?" he demanded.

Ruckus and I both looked around wildly for Luther.

A door opened in the back behind the counter, and Luther came out with a floor mop in his hand.

"Luther, it's him!" I cried.

Ruckus hurried around the counter toward Luther with me right behind him.

Luther backed up a few steps, his eyes big. He lifted the mop with his left arm and held up the wet part in front of him. It wasn't a weapon, but it was all he had.

"I'm sorry that pitch killed your brother, Ruckus," Luther said in a calm voice. "I didn't mean to hit him."

"I don't care if you meant to or not," Ruckus said. "My brother's dead on account of you." He held up something in his hand and flicked it open.

A *switchblade.*

"Luther!" I crouched low, took the bayonet out of the case, and slid it hard over the floor to him. It bumped against his foot. He scooped it up and dropped the mop at his feet. I dropped the case on the floor.

"I told you I'd kill you, boy," Ruckus said to Luther.

It was weird hearing those words come out of his mouth because it wasn't a comic book and it wasn't a movie. It was real. He sounded mad and even a little bit sad.

Ruckus was dressed like any other guy, in old blue jeans and a T-shirt. But when he held up the knife and looked at Luther, his eyes were crazy. I started trembling.

"It wasn't Luther's fault," I shouted. "He threw a good pitch."

Luther glanced at me and back at Ruckus. "Charlie," he said, "you get out of here, you hear me?"

"My brother raised me," Ruckus said. I knew if Luther didn't have Dad's bayonet, Ruckus would've rushed him by now.

He took a step toward Luther.

"Leave him alone!" I hollered. I wasn't so sure that

Luther would use that blade, even to defend himself.

But he *had* to. It was the only thing protecting him.

"Charlie," Luther said, "I'm tellin' you, son, get *out* of here."

I couldn't move. I wouldn't leave Luther for anything.

Ruckus moved to the side, and they circled each other. Luther didn't move the arm with the blade; he just held it out in front of him. The night was cool, but sweat ran in tiny rivers off his face.

Ruckus crept closer to Luther and Luther backed up a couple steps, still holding the bayonet blade out from his body. Three stacks of wooden egg crates sat just behind him. He bumped into them, and they crashed to the floor. Luther fell backwards on top of them, crushing a few crates and sending broken eggs sliding across the floor. He staggered to his feet, still holding the bayonet. The gooey eggs were slippery, and he slid to the floor again, landing on his back in the egg mess.

Ruckus rushed over and stomped on the hand Luther was using to hold the bayonet. Luther cried out and let go. Ruckus kicked it out of the way and bent over Luther with his switchblade.

I could see what was going to happen. So without thinking about it, I grabbed the nearest thing—one of the egg crates that wasn't broken—and smashed it over Ruckus's head as hard as I could.

He staggered a few steps, then hit the floor. He

wasn't unconscious, but he was stunned a little.

Luther scrambled for the bayonet and picked it up off the floor. I started toward Ruckus to yank the knife out of his hand, but Luther grabbed me around the waist and hoisted me in the air.

"Charlie, are you crazy, boy?" he yelled at me. "Let's get out of here!"

Chapter Sixteen

We were barely out the door when we heard the sirens. A squad car, red lights whirling, barreled up the street toward us and screeched to a stop outside Landen's. Two sheriff's deputies threw open their doors and leaped out, aiming guns at Luther.

"No! No!" I screamed, waving my arms. "Get Ruckus Brody—he's inside. He tried to kill Luther."

"He got a weapon?" It was Deputy Mead.

"A switchblade," I said.

They turned and walked with slow and careful steps into Landen's. A half minute later, one of them poked his head out of the screen door.

"We got 'im," the officer said. "Come inside, you two."

Me and Luther went inside Landen's.

The first two officers aimed guns at Ruckus, who still looked pretty dizzy from when I whacked him on the head. They had taken away his knife.

"Okay, tell us what happened," said Deputy Mead.

Just then, the screen door flew open and my mom and Vern rushed in.

"Charlie!" Mom cried. "What happened? Are you all right? We saw the police cars. Oh, Charlie!"

She threw her arms around me and held on real tight. Vern put his arm around her, but she didn't seem to notice. I tried to get away, but Mom was squeezing too hard.

"I'm okay," I said. She kept squishing me. "Let go, Mom, I can't breathe."

She finally let go.

Vern put a hand on my shoulder and I batted it away.

Deputy Mead cleared his throat. "Okay, suppose you all tell us what's goin' on?"

"He killed my brother," Ruckus said, pointing at Luther. His eyes looked clear now and focused sharp with hate.

"It was an accident!" I blurted out. I looked at Deputy Mead. "You know about what happened. And so does Sheriff Engle."

"That's right," the deputy said, nodding. "But I want to know what happened here tonight." He turned to Luther. "You tell me."

So Luther told him about how he'd come back to Landen's to clean. He told how Ruckus burst in, how I shoved the bayonet across the floor to him, and how they fought.

Mom gasped and held on to my shoulder. Vern still had his arm around her. Even with everything that had just happened, it burned me to see that.

Deputy Mead turned to Ruckus. "That pretty much what happened?"

"He killed my brother," Ruckus said.

"We're taking you in and charging you with assault," Deputy Mead said, slapping handcuffs over Ruckus's wrists. He looked at Luther. "And we'll need a formal statement from you, Mr. Peale."

Luther glanced around him. "Mr. Landen's depending on me to clean up this mess. Could I come in the morning? Or after I finish here?"

Mead nodded. "Okay, we'll get your statement in the morning. Meantime, you better call Landen and tell him what happened here."

One of the other deputies took down my address and Luther's address while Mom stood behind me, still gripping my shoulders.

When the deputies had all the information they wanted, they said we could go. The deputies walked Ruckus out the door, reading him his rights.

Luther held out Dad's bayonet to Mom. "Here, Mrs. Nebraska. I won't be needing this now."

"I'll take that," Vern said, stepping in front of Mom and grabbing the bayonet.

"Give it to Mom," I told him in a loud voice.

"Vern, I want to put that away," Mom said, her voice going as soft as mine was loud.

He glared at me but handed it over to her. She turned to me. "Where's the case?"

I picked the case up off the floor where I'd dropped it and handed it to her.

Luther turned to me. "Charlie, you shouldn't have done what you did. You could've got yourself killed. Now, I appreciate you comin' to help me, but it wasn't the right thing to do."

"Charlie," Mom said, "that man had a switchblade! Whatever were you thinking?"

"Luther didn't have nothin' to protect himself with," I said.

"Well, don't you worry about Ruckus, Charlie." Luther looked steady into my eyes. "He's goin' to jail now. Besides, we got a big game tomorrow." He put a hand on my shoulder and it felt pretty shaky, if you want to know the truth. But it sure felt better than Vern's fat paw. "You better go home and get rested so you can concentrate on that tomorrow."

"Okay," I said.

"Come on, Charlie," Vern said. "I'll drive you and your mom home."

I scowled at him. "I ain't goin' anywhere with you."

"Charlie—" Mom began.

"I'll walk home. I ain't ridin' with Vern."

Vern sighed loudly and ran a hand over the top of his head.

Mom said to Vern, "I'll walk home with Charlie. It's not that far."

"Mary, it's dark," he said, but Mom shook her head.

"Now that that man with the switchblade is going to jail, we'll be fine," she said. "Holden's a safe town. And I want to walk home with my son."

Vern glared at her, then at me. He walked out of

Landen's and let the screen door bang shut behind him.

"Ready to go?" Mom asked me. I nodded. "Good night, Luther."

"'Night, ma'am," he said. "'Night, Charlie. See you tomorrow on the ball field."

"Yeah," I said. "See you."

Mom and I walked down the street for a long time without talking. I wondered what she was thinking, but she kept it to herself till we were almost home.

Finally she said, "Charlie, I want you to know that I think you were very brave," she said. "But don't ever, *ever* do anything so dangerous again. You were wrong to take the bayonet when I told you not to. You could have been killed. Promise me you won't do anything like that again."

I kept walking and didn't say nothing. I knew if Luther ever needed help again, I'd do just about anything.

"Promise me, Charlie."

I sighed. "I promise."

It was a lie. But I thought maybe with Ruckus in jail, I wouldn't have to do anything dangerous again.

Chapter Seventeen

I was glad Ruckus was in jail. Mom said he'd probably have to go before a judge in Cedar Rapids. Then
maybe they'd take him back on the train to the sheriff in Tennessee.

I just wanted Ruckus far away from Luther so he
couldn't try to hurt him again. I had to talk Luther
out of going home. How would he be able to stay away
from Ruckus in Tennessee? But we still had to play
that game against Lobo and Will and the Wildcats. I'd
have to talk to him later.

It was weird thinking about Will in the same cate-
gory as Lobo and the Wildcats. What would it be like
to play a game against him? We'd always rooted for
each other. This time we'd be hoping the other guy
would make mistakes. In some ways, playing against
Will would be almost as hard as playing against Lobo.

Luther was a great coach, and we'd all improved a
lot. But I didn't think we'd improved enough to be
much competition for the Wildcats.

Lobo was still bragging that he was going to pitch against us. That made me more nervous than ever. Our concentration would have to be like Superman's not to let Lobo's sneer affect our hitting.

The morning started out sunny, but by noon, dark clouds rolled in. The man on the radio said it might rain in the afternoon. To tell you the truth, I hoped it would start pouring, but that didn't make a lot of sense. If the game was rained out, we'd just have to play it later. And Luther was leaving Holden soon. I sure didn't want to play this game without him around. So we might as well get it over with.

Mom dropped me off at the park at one and said she'd be back before two. She had some errands to run, she said. I hoped picking up Vern wasn't one of those errands, but I didn't ask her. I didn't want to get mad seeing the two of them up there in the stands but I didn't want to get all worked up now before the game.

The rest of the Stumptown Stormers got to the ball field at one o'clock, too.

"Lobo's gonna pitch for sure," Eileen said when we'd gathered around Luther. "I heard one of his friends talkin' about it."

Everyone groaned.

"It'll be hard for us to hit with Lobo makin' all those mean faces right from the pitcher's mound," Kathleen said.

"You remember what I told you the first day about

concentration?" Luther asked. "If you concentrate, you won't even see his face." He smiled. "But I had a feeling that Lobo might want to pitch."

We all looked at each other like it was doomsday.

"All right, Stormers, listen up," Luther said. "Having Lobo pitch is *good.*"

"What do ya mean, Luther?" Walter asked. "How could that be good?"

"Pitching isn't like playin' catch," Luther said. "Lobo's expecting to come here and get an easy win. But we'll use our speed and our ability to drag bunt. You all did a good job with that yesterday. The drag bunt'll surprise and frustrate him, especially when he pitches out of a stretch. We might not be able to hit Lobo, but we can bunt anybody. We need to put the ball in play and let Lobo's team make the mistakes."

Could that really work? A look around at my friends' faces showed me that pretty much everybody on the team was wondering the same thing.

But it was worth a try. We had to trust Luther. He'd worked his magic with us before. I just hoped his plan was good enough that we'd survive the game.

Luther unfolded a sheet of paper and read off the starting lineup. Eileen would be first at bat, then Devin, then me. I was real happy that Luther trusted me to bat third, but it made me even more scared. Alan would be next, in the cleanup spot.

The Wildcats boys began arriving before too long. Will came, too, but he didn't look at me. I didn't really care. I wondered if he knew that Luther had gotten dragged down to the sheriff's office after Will spilled the beans about what happened in Tennessee.

About twenty minutes before the game, a whole bunch of people started coming to the park. By five minutes to game time, the bleachers were packed, and folks were sitting around in lawn chairs. Most of the parents from both teams were there, and lots of people from town came to watch, too. It was the biggest crowd I'd ever seen at a baseball game.

Mom came alone and sat with Eileen's mom and dad. I was real happy she hadn't brought Vern with her.

When Coach Hennessey arrived, I got even more nervous. He leaned against the batter's cage, chewing a wad of gum.

Lobo got there at the last minute, strutting onto the ball field a little before two o'clock. He looked real sure of himself.

"You girls ready to get stomped on?" Lobo asked, grinning at us. He didn't look at me. I wondered if he was remembering how I'd seen his brother slap him at the A&P.

But then his ugly mouth curled into a sneer that could've been peeled off the devil himself. "Prepare to die," Lobo told us.

"Come on, Charlie and Brad," Luther called. "Time for the coin toss."

I almost laughed out loud when Luther called Lobo "Brad." His first name didn't sound so scary that way.

And I could see by the way Lobo's face got all red that he didn't like being called Brad.

Lobo, me, and Luther met at home plate for the coin toss to decide the home team. Luther flipped the quarter into the air.

"You call it, Brad," Luther said.

"Heads," Lobo yelled.

It came up heads, so us Stormers would be up at bat first. Me and Luther and the rest of the team hustled to our places for hitting.

A raindrop fell on my nose. I hadn't noticed till then that the sky had gotten darker. Maybe we'd get rained out after all. "Remember our strategy," Luther told us in a low voice, and we all nodded.

"Go, Stumptown!" some of the parents yelled from the stands, clapping. "You can do it!"

Eileen was up first. She's left-handed, so she stood on the right side of the plate in a good, closed position.

Lobo snorted. "They're puttin' a *girl* first?" he called out. "Get ready for the game's first strikeout."

He wound up and threw a powerful fastball.

Eileen did the drag bunt just perfect. The second the ball left Lobo's hand, she swiveled fast from a closed position to an open one. She let the ball bounce hard off the very end of the bat and took off for first base before Lobo knew what was what.

Lobo was so surprised by the drag bunt, he scrambled for the ball and fell on his face. By the time he was back on his feet and scooped up the ball, Eileen was safe at first.

We all grinned, and a ripple of laughter ran through the crowd of Stormers fans. The drag bunt had worked! It was the last thing Lobo had expected, and he'd blown the play.

The laughing made Lobo's shame worse, and he got red in the face. He was pacing around the pitcher's mound and he looked like he was grinding his teeth, too.

Alan gave me a thumbs-up, and I blew out a relieved sigh. Luther smiled at me and nodded.

I glanced at Will. He was looking real serious. Was he wishing he'd played on our side?

A few more soft raindrops sprinkled around us now. The air had a good earthy smell, but I wasn't thinking about that too much. I didn't want to get rained out now. After getting our first base hit, I hoped we'd be able to play for a while. I was curious to see if Luther's strategy would keep working.

Next up was Devin.

"Concentrate, Lobo!" Coach Hennessey hollered from the stands.

Our team had to concentrate, too. One good play was a start, but we had a long way to go.

Lobo pitched another hardball to Devin. Devin bunted, too, only he used a regular bunt, which surprised Lobo all over again. Lobo fielded it and threw to second, but Eileen was already safe.

The people in the stands on our side stood up and cheered wildly.

Lobo was rattled, that was for sure. And after all his bragging and strutting, the surprise plays made it all the worse for him. He stomped around, muttering words I couldn't hear.

Now it was my turn at bat. I tried to fill my mind with all Luther had taught me about hitting. I kept my focus glued on that baseball in Lobo's hand, and I whispered to myself, "I'm gonna hit the ball. I'm gonna hit it."

I kept myself in a closed position and took my stance. I was ready.

Lobo wound up and threw a powerful pitch. I swung and smashed the ball with all the strength I had. It flew out over the first baseman's head and into right field.

"You got it, Charlie!" Luther hollered. "You got it!"

I ran all the way to third base, following Eileen and Devin, who safely made it home.

Half the crowd in the stands cheered and clapped. I grinned at Luther and he held up a fist, beaming. Will glanced at me a second and turned away again.

I wanted Will to be impressed with our team and Luther's coaching. I'm not sure why I cared about that, but I did.

The game was going real good. In fact, now I wanted it to go on and on. Luther had performed some kind of magic on us, all right. We were holding our own against the mighty Wildcats!

I knew I'd be up to pitch soon. Then I remembered

I'd left my bag of rosin in the car. If it didn't stop sprinkling, the ball would be slippery, and I'd be sure to need it.

Alan stepped up to bat. He was a great choice for the cleanup spot, because he was a powerful hitter. Lobo, still grinding his teeth, wound up and threw. Alan hit it toward Lobo. Lobo bobbled the ball and threw to first, but way over the first baseman's head.

I slid in for my first run of the game. Lobo threw his cap on the ground and stomped all over the pitcher's mound. The Stumptown fans went crazy, whistling and hollering.

Coach Hennessey strode onto the field with long, angry steps and called a team meeting. The Wildcats crowded around Hennessey for a minute while he talked to them.

What were they going to do? I looked at Luther, and he winked at me. Lobo's team seemed shocked that we already had three runs on them. The Wildcats' parents and the folks in the stands who wanted to see us lose looked pretty unhappy, too. Some of them were grumbling loudly about Hennessey and Lobo.

Out on the field, Hennessey pointed at Lobo's chest and said something.

"What?" Lobo yelled.

Hennessey gave a nod. Then he turned his back on Lobo and walked off the field to his spot by the batter's cage. Lobo stomped from the pitcher's mound to third base.

Hennessey had *fired* Lobo as pitcher!

We Stormers couldn't stop grinning. No matter who won the game, we had already beat Brad Lobo. Maybe that would knock him down a peg or two. Or ten. I sure hoped so.

It was still sprinkling, so I figured I'd better go to the car and get my rosin. It looked like I'd be pitching the next inning.

I hurried to Mom's car in the parking lot behind the stands and found my bag of rosin on the front seat where I'd left it. I slammed the door shut and was heading back through the parking lot when somebody grabbed me from behind. A hand clapped over my mouth.

"I don't want to hurt you, kid, so just stay calm."

Ruckus Brody.

I stifled a scream.

My body started to shake. *How did he get out of jail?*

He let go and gave me a little shove.

I glanced back to see a knife in his fist. A different one from last night, but it looked just as mean.

I walked in front of him, feeling hot and then cold with the thoughts that tore through my head. Would he kill Luther? Could I help Luther this time? I didn't have the bayonet. I didn't have nothing that could help him. I felt bad, almost sick, I was so scared for Luther.

I started toward the ball field, but Ruckus grabbed my arm and jerked me in another direction.

"This way," he said. "I want him to see you from a ways off."

"How'd you get out of jail?" I asked, walking ahead of him.

"Friend of your mom's. Her boyfriend, I guess."

I whirled around. "You mean *Vern Jardine?* Vern bailed you out of jail?"

"Keep walkin', kid," he said, and shoved me again. I did what he said. "Yeah, that's him. Vern Jardine and a couple others. Luther seems to've made himself some enemies up here, too."

I'll kill Vern, I thought. *If anything happens to Luther, I swear, I'll kill him.* I think at that moment I hated Vern even more than Ruckus.

"See that bench? Head out there," Ruckus said.

I kept walking. The tree was maybe fifty yards from the ball field. When we got to the bench, Ruckus said, "Sit down."

I sat, the tiny puddles of rain on the bench soaking through my pants. "You're the bait that'll get Luther over here," Ruckus said. "So you sit there and look over at him, and wait till he sees you."

What if Mom sees us first? I thought. *She'd get help from somebody real fast.*

I sure hoped so.

The game was still going on, even though it was raining harder now. Luther stood next to the backstop, watching the game. I wondered how long it would take him to notice I was gone.

I sat there, trying to figure out how to warn Luther, to tell him Ruckus was here and to get away. But I knew Luther wouldn't run. If he saw me here with Ruckus, he'd try to help me.

And maybe he'd die because of it.

It was Walter who finally spotted me. He walked around the backstop and stood next to Luther. Then he waved. "Hey, Charlie!" he hollered at me. "What're you doin' way over there?"

Luther turned and saw me and Ruckus. Even from that far away, I could see his body stiffen. He said something to Walter, then started walking fast toward me and Ruckus.

"You just do what I told you now," Ruckus said. He shifted his knife from one hand to the other.

"He's my best friend," I said, real quiet.

When Luther was halfway to us, he called out, "You okay, Charlie?"

"He's got a knife, Luther!" I yelled, waving my arms. "Go back!"

But Luther didn't go back. He didn't even slow down. He just kept walking toward us.

"Good boy," Ruckus told Luther under his breath.

Luther stopped right in front of us. The rain was still coming down steady, plopping on his head, sliding down his face, soaking his clothes. He blinked rain out of his eyes.

"Let Charlie go," Luther said. "This is between me and you."

"That's just what I had in mind," Ruckus said. "Get out of here, kid."

I didn't move.

Luther jerked his head toward the ball field. "Go back, Charlie. They're about to call the game 'cause of the rain. You played real good, son."

A buzzing sound came loud in my ear, and I shooed a hornet away.

A hornet? I looked up. That hornet's nest was right above us in the tree.

"Charlie!" It was Mom. She was over at the ball field, staring at me and hopping from one foot to the other. I'm sure she recognized Ruckus, because she was screaming her head off. "Charlie! Oh, somebody help Charlie!"

I guess nobody moved fast enough, so she started running toward us.

I spotted a couple of rocks on the ground, about the size of an egg, and an idea filled my mind. I reached down and scooped up the rocks.

I'm gonna hit that nest, I'm gonna hit it. I focused real hard and fired the rocks, one after another, into the tree.

Both rocks hit the nest. Maybe a dozen hornets sprayed out of it and flew wild around us. Ruckus batted at them and swore, dropping the knife.

I grabbed Luther's shirt. "Come on!" I yelled. He was getting stung all over his neck and arms, even more than me.

Mom was still running toward us.

I turned and screamed, "Mom, go back! *Go back!*"

"Come on!" I yelled again at Luther. Me and Luther took off running across the wet grass in the rain.

"This way to the sheriff's office?" he shouted at me.

"Yeah," I hollered back. "Follow me!"

We headed off through the park. I could hear another set of footsteps pounding the ground.

Ruckus was chasing us, and he wasn't far behind.

Chapter Eighteen

Me and Luther flew over the ground across the park. The rain was hammering us hard now. With every pounding step on the soggy grass, water splashed out in every direction.

I didn't have to look back. I could hear Ruckus running behind us, his breath coming in ragged gasps.

The sheriff's office was six or seven blocks away.

Maybe we'd see somebody on the street who could help us. Maybe they'd give us a ride. Or let us come inside and phone the sheriff.

But who else helped bail Ruckus out of jail? I knew we could trust some people, but there were others I wasn't so sure about.

I glanced over at Luther. He was holding his bad arm close to his side instead of pumping it to help him run. Rain was streaming down his face.

We came to the street at the edge of the park and hardly slowed down. We tore across it with no cars in sight. I guess everybody wanted to stay dry inside.

There was nobody to yell to for help.

We kept running.

I was getting tired, and I could tell Luther was, too, but we couldn't slow down now. Not with Ruckus chasing us. Not until we got to the sheriff's office.

I saw the library off to our right, and that gave me an idea.

"Come on," I yelled to Luther. "Maybe we can lose him."

We ran up the steps to the front door, pulled it open, and rushed into the building.

Mrs. Crawford sat at the circulation desk, stamping books. She frowned over her reading glasses as we ran toward her.

"Charlie, what on earth—?"

"Call the sheriff, Mrs. Crawford," I said breathlessly. I pushed Luther past the card catalogs. "And if a man comes in after us, tell him we went out that way." I pointed to the door leading to the alley at the side.

She stood up, leaned across the desk, and peered at me. "Tell *who* you went that way, Charlie? What man?"

I didn't have time to answer. I ran ahead of Luther and led him up the stairs to the second floor loft.

A little boy about three stood next to his mother, who was searching through the shelves. He had a lollipop or something in his mouth that gave him a chipmunk cheek. He watched us as we ducked behind the stack of books closest to the railing. I slid a few books to the side so we could see the main floor.

Ruckus ran in the front door, breathing heavy. He was soaked from the rain. Water ran off him and made a giant puddle around his feet. He stood in the middle of the floor, looking around.

I could see his knife. He'd tucked it into his belt.

Mrs. Crawford came around the circulation desk, watching him.

Please, Mrs. Crawford, don't let on we're up here, I told her silently.

"Excuse me, sir," Mrs. Crawford said to Ruckus.

He circled around the card catalogs.

"Sir?" Mrs. Crawford moved a step closer. "May I help you?"

"Just looking," Ruckus said.

His face tilted up then, and he saw the loft. "How do I get up there?" he asked, pointing.

"Maybe I can..." Mrs. Crawford said, but Ruckus saw the exit sign over the door into the stairwell. He laid a hand over the knife in his belt and headed for the steps.

He was coming for us. Even in the public library.

Luther yanked on my shirt and jerked his head sideways like he wanted me to follow him. We hurried to the far end of the stacks. We turned, went down two more stacks, and ducked between the shelves.

I looked down and caught my breath. We were as wet as Ruckus and leaving a wet trail on the floor. If Ruckus looked down, he'd see the water and follow the footprints right to us.

There was nothing around to dry our shoes. I nudged Luther and pointed to the wet spots under our feet.

Footsteps pounded up the stairs and shuffled into the loft.

"What are you looking for, sir?" I could hear Mrs. Crawford's voice. "Maybe I can help."

She'd come upstairs behind Ruckus. She was talking unusually loud for a librarian.

Luther pushed his hand into a pocket and came up with his old bandanna. He dried the bottoms of my feet, then his.

Then he pulled me through two more rows. The floor was dry now under our feet.

The little kid suddenly appeared at the end of the stack, about ten feet away, and stared at us. I put my finger to my lips, hoping he'd keep quiet. He didn't say anything but held the lollipop up for me to take a lick. I shook my head no.

"Come on, Nate," his mother called from the other side of the loft. "Time to go."

The little boy glanced toward his mom, then us. He must've decided that we weren't all that interesting, because he turned away and took off running.

There was another sudden rush of footsteps. They came from where we'd just been standing, drying our feet.

"Surely I can help you," Mrs. Crawford's voice called. "If you'll just tell me what you're looking for."

I remembered the back room that Mr. Billet had walked out of the last time I was here. I nudged Luther.

Let the door be unlocked. Please.

I twisted the doorknob and it turned. We quietly went inside and closed the door. I pushed in the lock button and put my ear to the door.

"Where'd they go?" Ruckus asked.

"Where did *who* go?" Mrs. Crawford asked.

Mrs. Crawford was a pretty good actress. She sounded like she had no idea who he was looking for. Ruckus was probably suspicious, though, that a librarian would follow him all the way upstairs when he didn't want her help.

Footsteps shuffled a little closer. "What's in there?" he asked.

He was asking about this room.

"It's a workroom," she answered. "I'm sorry, but that's just for library employees, and..."

The doorknob rattled, and I jumped back a couple of feet.

"We keep that room locked," Mrs. Crawford said casually.

"There was a boy and a colored fella," Ruckus said. "They were here. See the footprints back there?"

"There have been a lot of people up here since it started raining. I—" She stopped short. "Oh, I think I know who you mean. Are those two friends of yours? They *were* here. They rushed in but rushed out right away."

"Where'd they go?" Ruckus asked.

"Outside. They probably didn't get far. If you go down the stairs and out the side door, you may be able to catch them."

His heavy footsteps rushed off, tromped down the stairs, and finally faded away.

Luther and I waited a few more seconds.

"It's okay now, Charlie." Mrs. Crawford's voice was muffled and low.

Luther nodded at me, and I pulled open the door.

"Thanks, Mrs. Crawford," I said.

"What's going on, Charlie?" she asked. "Who was that character?"

Her eyebrows bunched up. She looked back and forth at me and Luther over her glasses.

"That was Ruckus Brody," I said. "He's after Luther."

Her eyes widened. "I think we should call the sheriff," she said.

I didn't remind her that I'd suggested that when we first ran into the library.

I said to Luther, "Yeah, let's wait here for the sheriff to come."

"We're not far from the sheriff's office, are we?" Luther asked. "Just a couple of blocks?"

"Right," I said. "About three blocks."

"Okay," Luther said. "You point the way, so I remember where it is. Then you wait here. I'll go myself. I want me and you separated till Ruckus is rounded up."

"No," I said. "We're staying together."

"I'm not listening to an argument, Charlie," Luther said, his voice louder.

I opened my mouth to argue, but he put up his hand.

"I said I'm not listenin'."

"Charlie, you stay here," Mrs. Crawford said. "Besides, you're soaking wet."

"So is Luther," I pointed out.

"Charlie," Luther said, his eyes blazing now. "You're *not* leaving with me."

I could see his mind was set.

"Okay, okay," I said. "Let's walk outside, and I'll show you which way to go."

We said good-bye to Mrs. Crawford, who hadn't stopped frowning over her glasses, and went outside. It was still raining hard.

Luther looked down the street. "It's this way, isn't it?"

"Down to the corner, turn left, and it's two more blocks on the right. The big brick building."

"Okay, I remember now," Luther said. "Thanks, Charlie." He reached out and squeezed my shoulder. "I'll see you later."

I heard running footsteps and looked over to see someone running this way.

"Luther, it's Ruckus," I said.

He was down the block and running toward us, but he was between us and the sheriff's office. He must have figured out that Luther and I hadn't left the library.

"This way! Hurry!" I grabbed Luther's arm and pulled. He pulled back for half a second. But then he nodded, and we started running again.

Now we were headed in the wrong direction, away from the sheriff's office.

With Ruckus Brody close behind.

Chapter Nineteen

We'll have to double back!" I yelled at Luther.

We ran past Jennings Bookstore, Martin's Florist and Garden Supply, Hanson's Quilt Shop, and then away from downtown.

By now the rain had turned into a full-fledged storm. The sky looked like a painting done by some angry artist, swirled in a mess of gray and black. A jag of lightning cut through the darkness. Then came the thunder like a big bass drum that rolled louder and louder, finally crashing in our ears.

We were running toward the Red Cedar River. I knew its path and figured we could find a place, maybe in the woods, that would let us cut back without Ruckus seeing us.

I hoped.

I heard a squeal of tires and looked back just in time to see Ruckus bounce off the hood of a car in the street. He landed in the middle of the road, stumbled, and fell to his knees.

"Stop, Luther!" I yelled. "Ruckus was hit by a car."
We stopped and turned to watch.

The driver jerked to a stop and leaped out of the
car. "Are you all right?" the man yelled.

Ruckus didn't answer. He staggered to his feet,
pulled the knife out of his belt, and started running
toward us again.

So we took off.

"Hey!" the driver yelled to Ruckus. "Are you crazy?
What's the matter with you?"

We ran through the woods and down the embank-
ment next to the river. We didn't let up as the heavy
rain kept pouring down. My lungs felt like they might
explode.

I'd been to this place more than a hundred times.
The storm sewer was down there. Its huge round
opening looked like a giant hippo's yawn, frozen in
cement.

Me and Luther got to the bottom of the slope. The
ground was mushy under our feet and sucked us down
so we couldn't run good.

I'd made a mistake. I should've kept us on higher
ground.

I looked up to see Ruckus in the woods at the top of
the slope. He spotted us and came—slipping and sliding in the mud—down the hill. He had the knife in his
hand, and I saw the blade pop out.

Luther saw it too. "We gotta split up here," he said,
giving me a little push. "You go that way. Do it, Charlie."

"No." I wouldn't leave him for anything.

Luther's eyes were pleading. "Charlie, you have to go."

The opening of the storm sewer—the tunnel under the streets of Holden—stood there like it was inviting us in.

Water swirled out, but it wasn't deep. We could disappear into it, come out a half block away, and run back to the sheriff's office.

"Come on," I said. "I'll show you the way."

Luther hesitated for half a second, then followed me into the storm sewer. The water was cold and rushed around us at our ankles. It pushed against our feet, making it hard to walk.

"We got to hurry to the first manhole," I said to Luther, over my shoulder. "The water'll be rising with all this rain."

We went about ten yards into the tunnel to the place where it first gets smaller. The top of the sewer was now only a couple of feet above Luther's head.

The easiest way to move was by pulling my knees up high so my feet came out of the water. It was the fastest way, too.

Luther grabbed my wrist with his good hand.

"I'll go first," he said. "Hold my wrist, and don't let go."

I wrapped my fingers around his wrist and held on. We splashed farther into the blackness, linked together, with Luther staying just ahead of me.

Then I heard splashing and huffing behind us. Sure enough, it was Ruckus. All I could make out was his silhouette and the gray light behind him. He was moving fast, hopping through the water as it surged toward the river.

The tunnel suddenly got smaller again, and the rounded part above us just brushed the top of Luther's head. That squeezed the water higher on us. It was up to my waist now, pushing us back toward Ruckus. Luther pulled me closer and grabbed me around my waist.

We were about halfway to the manhole, I figured, and the water was rising fast. It hit me then that there was no turning back. We didn't have a weapon against Ruckus. We had to make it to the manhole. The water was so cold, I started shivering. The tunnel smelled of rain and the dust and dirt that gets washed along the street before it dumps into the storm sewer.

"How far?" Luther yelled over the noise of the pounding water. We passed a side tunnel where the water gushed into the main tunnel. If Luther didn't have a tight hold on me, it would've knocked me over.

"Quarter of a block," I yelled. My voice didn't sound like me. It was gaspy and scared. "There'll be a light above us. The manhole's at that light."

Why did I take us here? I thought. *We'll never make it.* The water was rising too fast. Going this way, we'd drown. Going back the other way, we'd be killed by Ruckus.

Luther pushed on. He still held his right arm close, his good arm wrapped around me. That bad arm—and me—slowed us down.

Suddenly the water rose again. It swirled around my chest. I tried to help by dog-paddling, but it didn't do much.

I was scareder than I'd ever been in my life, and I was shaking all over. I was sure we were going to die.

I squinted into the blackness ahead of us. A tiny light flashed up ahead. Then I knew. It was lightning, blinking a pinpoint of brightness into the dark world underground.

And it came through the manhole cover!

"There it is!" I yelled. "Up ahead." We must've gone farther than I'd thought.

"Sweet Jesus, thank you," Luther whispered.

The water swirled around his neck, and he held me up to keep my head above water. He could hardly move now, and Ruckus was only a few yards behind us. We were all like snails, moving in slow motion.

The manhole was just a foot away now.

"Grab the iron bar," I hollered. "Overhead."

He boosted me high. "*You* grab it," he yelled.

I got hold of it and turned to Luther. The water was over his mouth. His head was tilted back to keep his nose out of the water.

"Come on!" I yelled. "There's room for us both." I pulled myself up onto the second iron bar and pushed against the manhole cover. It didn't budge.

I didn't know if it was stuck or if I was just too tired to push it up.

"I can't!" I screamed. "It's stuck!"

Luther pulled himself up with his good arm and hooked that elbow over the iron bar. Then he pushed his shoulder against the manhole cover and shoved it out.

Beautiful gray light and rain and fresh air poured over us.

A hand suddenly grabbed my leg. Ruckus was just under me, holding on, his head tipped back trying to keep his face above water. He yanked on me hard, and I slipped off the top iron bar.

"Luther!"

Luther was still holding tight to the bar with his good hand. So he reached down with the other hand—the *weak* one—grabbed me, and yanked me up.

I kicked at Ruckus as hard as I could, and he let go. With Luther still holding me, we climbed out of the manhole together. Hayes School stood in the fog across the field. I was so tired, I collapsed on the grass.

Luther turned and leaned back into the storm sewer. He reached down for Ruckus, who was struggling in the water.

"Take my hand!" Luther hollered.

My kick had thrown Ruckus back a step. He was a foot away now from the iron bar and Luther's hand. Ruckus reached up for the iron bar, but a sudden rush of water surged over his head.

He disappeared.

"Ruckus!" Luther shouted. "Ruckus!"

All we could hear was the swoosh of water storming through the tunnel. It filled all the space, leaving no air for him to breathe. It swept everything in its path back toward the river.

Ruckus was gone.

Chapter Twenty

They found Ruckus Brody's body two days later. A fisherman spotted him more than a half mile downriver from the entrance to the storm sewer. We got the news just before supper when Sheriff Engle called Mom.

Me and Luther were sitting on the davenport in the living room while the potatoes cooked. Mom came back from the telephone, sat down in the rocker, and told us that Ruckus had been found. Luther hung his head.

"You tried to save him, Luther," I said. "You told him to grab your hand."

"But I didn't save him."

"Luther," Mom said, leaning forward, "he was a bad man. He died trying to kill you and Charlie, and you tried to save his life. You're not responsible for Ruckus's death. You're a hero."

She got up from the rocking chair and went over to him. "I'm so glad you came into our lives, Luther," she said. She put her arms around him and gave him a hug.

Luther looked surprised but pleased. He patted Mom's shoulder in an awkward way.

She pulled back and sat down next to him. "I'm so embarrassed and furious about Vern and those men bailing Ruckus out of jail. Luther, I can't tell you how sorry I am."

"It wasn't your fault, Mrs. Nebraska," Luther said. "You didn't know they were gonna do that."

"The phone's been ringing off the wall," Mom said. "Everyone wants to know how you two are. The whole town has heard what happened by now. Luther, a few of them called to say they want you to know they're sorry about how you've been treated here in Holden."

Luther nodded, looking serious.

"Mom, you aren't gonna see Vern again, are you?" I asked.

"No, absolutely not," Mom said. "I told that man never to come over here, never to call me, ever again. Anyone who'd do the horrible thing he did—well, we'll never have to see him again, Charlie."

"Good," I said.

It took a load off my mind to know that Vern was out of our lives for good. Now Mom and I could go back to living the way we did before she met him.

Not exactly, though. Knowing Luther had changed me in ways that weren't real clear in my mind. But for sure the Will and baseball and Brad Lobo parts of my life were different now.

In some ways, it seemed like I met Luther a year ago instead of just a few weeks.

During the last couple of days, I'd thought a lot about Dad. He wasn't coming home. It had surprised me when that thought floated in and settled in my mind. But I didn't panic.

I'd turned it around and looked at it from all sides.

He wasn't going to come walking through that front door again, calling my name. And all the wishing and hoping in the world wouldn't make that happen.

Luther told me that day down by the river that Dad could live on forever if I keep him alive inside of me. So I'll think about him every day and talk to him whenever I feel like it. Maybe he'll be listening.

"Luther, how's your arm feeling?" Mom asked.

Luther shook his head. "I don't understand it, Mrs. Nebraska. That arm didn't work for months, till Charlie needed help. The doctor told me that can happen sometimes. He had a name for it, but I don't recall it. He said I must have been feelin' so bad about killing a person with my pitching arm it just stopped working for a while. But when Charlie was in trouble, I guess I forgot about it. I didn't even know what happened till Charlie told me later. It's weak, but I can build up the strength. I hope I'll even be able to pitch again someday."

"That would be wonderful," Mom said. She sighed. "Life sure has a way of changing fast." She looked at me. "Charlie, I've been thinking. I want to go back to school."

My mouth dropped open, I was so surprised. "Really?"

"Yes. Maybe I'll learn how to be a beautician. I could make more money cutting ladies' hair than working the cash register at Woolworth's. We'll have to tighten our belts a bit, but we've still got your dad's pension. You think we could live on less money for a while?"

"Sure," I said, shrugging. "I don't need nothin'."

"Anything."

I rolled my eyes. "Anything."

Mom smiled. "Thanks, honey." She looked back and forth between me and Luther. "Well, I better check those potatoes." She got up and walked into the kitchen.

"So," Luther said, "I hear Coach Hennessey wants you to play with the Wildcats. You musta really impressed him."

"Yeah," I said. "Will called me, too. He said he was sorry for telling why you came up here to Iowa. But I'm the one who blabbed to Will in the first place. You wouldn't have had all that trouble if I hadn't—"

"Charlie," Luther interrupted. "Stop right there. You weren't to blame for anything."

Luther was just being nice. I knew I was to blame for a *lot* of what happened. But I was glad Will called to say he was sorry for his part. I don't know what'll happen between him and me. Maybe we'll be friends again someday. Maybe not.

"So you gonna play with the Wildcats now?" Luther asked.

"No," I said. "It made me feel pretty good that Coach Hennessey wants me on the team, but I told him I was playin' with the Stumptown Stormers. He's an okay coach, I guess, but you're miles better at teaching us."

Luther looked at the floor a second, then back up at me.

"Charlie," he said, kind of slow. "Remember what I said about goin' back home? I don't have to worry about Ruckus no more, you know."

Something pressed on my chest. "I was afraid you'd say that."

"I called Mr. Landen and gave him my notice this morning."

"But, Luther..." A knot appeared in my throat. "What about our team? What about—about me and you and—"

"Charlie," he said, leaning toward me. "I'm sure grateful I got you for a friend. If I was to have a boy of my own one day, I hope he'll be just like you. But I want to be near my family—"

"But *we're* like a family," I said. "Me and you—and Mom."

"That's right, we are," he said. "But I got another family who misses me, and I got to get home. Besides, I'm gonna get this arm back in shape. I want to play ball again, and I think I got a good chance with the minors. Maybe even the majors. The Negro League's disappearing now. Ever since Jackie got into the

National League, more colored men are playin' major league ball."

"Hey, yeah," I said, starting to feel a little better. "You could be a baseball star. You got that powerful pitch. Maybe I could listen to your games on the radio."

Luther smiled. "We'll see. It'd be good to get back to playin' again." He looked at me steady for a second or two. "I'll miss you, Charlie Nebraska. Maybe you could come visit me one day, you and your mama. I could meet you at the train."

"That'd be great, Luther."

"We had a good time, didn't we?"

"Yeah," I said. "We sure did."

"And you're right, Charlie. We *are* like a family."

"Yeah."

He was quiet for a second. Then he said, "I love you, son."

I opened my mouth, but no words came out. So I pitched myself into him and held on for a real long time.

About the Authors

CAROL GORMAN is the author of many books for young readers, including books about Jerry Flack, who first appeared in *Dork in Disguise*. That title was chosen for children's choice lists in nine states and was named the winner in Missouri, Oklahoma, South Carolina, Washington, and West Virginia. Her novels have been published in seven countries and translated into four languages. She is frequently invited to make author appearances and in the past few years has spoken to more than 10,000 teachers, librarians, and students across the country. She and her husband Ed, a mystery writer, live in Cedar Rapids, Iowa, where Carol also teaches at Coe College. Readers may visit her website at *www.carolgorman.com*.

RON J. FINDLEY has been involved in baseball since he was a boy growing up in Cedar Rapids, Iowa. As a child, he says, he was always looking for a sandlot baseball game, and many of the ideas for *Stumptown Kid* are based on his memories of that time. In his teens he was the starting centerfielder for Jefferson High School. In 1961, his undefeated team became the Iowa High School State Baseball Champions. Ron played at the highest level in Men's Major Fastpitch Softball, and he founded the Iowa Fastpitch Softball Hall of Fame. He coached youth football, baseball, and softball teams for many years. Ron has two grown children and five grandchildren.